"You want a hit? Totally legal, you know." Geoff grinned over at Ford as Angie and Hetty looked more like they were fixin' to die.

"Hell, yes. I only share if you do." Ford came over and sat on a hay bale.

"That's totally fair." Stoney refused to act all freaked. He tried to snatch the doobie from Angie's fingers so he could offer it over, but Geoff got hold of it first.

"You're not going to offer him a shotgun, boss?"

He was going to kill Geoff. Especially when Ford lit up like Christmas.

"Makes me cough less that way," Ford pointed out, and butter wouldn't melt in Ford's mouth.

"Well, I sure as shit won't let anyone else do it." Wait. Did he say that out loud?

Geoff chortled, handing over the joint, and yeah, he was going to do this. Ford leaned close, eyes closing, lashes dark on his cheeks.

Stoney took a deep hit and leaned forward. As he did, he heard Ford pass the bag of candy off to someone.

Then their lips met.

Welcome to
Dreamspun Desires

Dear Reader,

Love is the dream. It dazzles us, makes us stronger, and brings us to our knees. Dreamspun Desires tell stories of love featuring your favorite heartwarming heroes, captivating plots, and exotic locations. Stories that make your breath catch and your imagination soar.

In the pages of these wonderful love stories, readers can escape to a world where love conquers all, the tenderness of a first kiss sweeps you away, and your heart pounds at the sight of the one you love.

When you put it all together, you find romance in its truest form.

Love always finds a way.

Elizabeth North

Executive Director
Dreamspinner Press

BA Tortuga

Commitment Ranch

Published by

Published by
DREAMSPINNER PRESS

5032 Capital Circle SW, Suite 2, PMB# 279,
Tallahassee, FL 32305-7886 USA
www.dreamspinnerpress.com

This is a work of fiction. Names, characters, places, and incidents either are the product of author imagination or are used fictitiously, and any resemblance to actual persons, living or dead, business establishments, events, or locales is entirely coincidental.

Commitment Ranch
© 2016 BA Tortuga.

Cover Art
© 2016 Bree Archer.
http://www.breearcher.com
Cover content is for illustrative purposes only and any person depicted on the cover is a model.

All rights reserved. This book is licensed to the original purchaser only. Duplication or distribution via any means is illegal and a violation of international copyright law, subject to criminal prosecution and upon conviction, fines, and/or imprisonment. Any eBook format cannot be legally loaned or given to others. No part of this book may be reproduced or transmitted in any form or by any means, electronic or mechanical, including photocopying, recording, or by any information storage and retrieval system, without the written permission of the Publisher, except where permitted by law. To request permission and all other inquiries, contact Dreamspinner Press, 5032 Capital Circle SW, Suite 2, PMB# 279, Tallahassee, FL 32305-7886, USA, or www.dreamspinnerpress.com.

ISBN: 978-1-63477-367-6
Digital ISBN: 978-1-63477-368-3
Library of Congress Control Number: 2016947413
Published September 2016
v. 1.0

Printed in the United States of America
∞
This paper meets the requirements of
ANSI/NISO Z39.48-1992 (Permanence of Paper).

BA TORTUGA, Texan to the bone and an unrepentant Daddy's Girl, spends her days with her basset hounds, getting tattooed, texting her sisters, and eating Mexican food. When she's not doing that, she's writing. She spends her days off watching rodeo, knitting, and surfing Pinterest in the name of research. BA's personal saviors include her wife, Julia Talbot, her best friend, Sean Michael, and coffee. Lots of coffee. Really good coffee.

Having written everything from fist fighting rednecks to hard-core cowboys to werewolves, BA does her damnedest to tell the stories of her heart, which was raised in Northeast Texas, but has heard the call of the high desert and lives in the Sandias. With books ranging from hard-hitting GLBT romance, to fiery ménages, to the most traditional of love stories, BA refuses to be pigeon-holed by anyone but the voices in her head.

Website: www.batortuga.com
Blog: batortuga.blogspot.com
Facebook: www.facebook.com/batortuga
Twitter: @batortuga

Chapter One

HIS phone rang somewhere around Leadville. Shit, Ford Nixel hadn't even known you could get cell signal in Leadville. He sure as hell didn't have any luck with the satellite radio, for Christ's sake. Thank God for hands-free stuff.

"Hello?"

"Ford? It's your Uncle Tyson."

"Hey, old man. How are you?"

"Your secretary said you were on your way up to Aspen. You think you could come on out to the ranch?"

Ford swerved a little in surprise, then pulled off at the next wide spot before he hurt something. "Well, hey, I can meet you in Glenwood if you want to have lunch at Juicy Lucy's."

He hadn't talked to Uncle Ty in person for… shit, three years? Maybe a little longer? He hadn't been to the ranch in twelve years, and he had no intention of breaking that record anytime soon.

"No, son, I need you to come. Please?"

Okay, whoa. In all these years, Ty had never once asked, not after they'd had a blowout of epic proportions, at any rate. Some things you never recovered from all the way. "Are you sick?"

When he didn't get an immediate response, he knew what the answer was, and he was glad he'd stopped the car.

"I'd rather talk to you in person, son. I haven't seen you. Can you come?"

Ford wanted to just shout a negative, but Ty had never asked him for a thing in his adult life. How could he refuse now? "Of course I can. I'm just out of Leadville, so it will be suppertime. Should I get something on the way in?"

"No. No. Geoff is making potato soup and biscuits for the guests. There will be plenty."

"Oh, you got a new cook?" Last time they'd sat down together, Ty's old housekeeper slash cook had gone to Florida.

"Stoney hired him a few years ago. He's a character and a half—a vegetarian that makes the best brisket on earth."

"No shit?" He leaned his head back against his seat. "Sounds like a hoot."

"He's something else, but a good guy. I'll have my guest room made up for you."

"Thanks." Oh, man, now he had to stay? Shit, this was bad. "I'll be there late this afternoon."

"I appreciate it, son. Genuinely."

"You know you can always call, Ty. I'll see you soon. Love you." Ford hung up, marveling about how he hadn't said those words to his uncle since he was at the ranch last, and that wasn't really fair, was it? He did love Ty fiercely.

If only the man hadn't taken in his jerk of an ex from college.

Ford shook his head, then keyed up his phone to call his assistant, Eileen, who worked at his office in Aspen.

"Good afternoon, sir. How's it going?"

Eileen was so professional. So smooth. Nothing like his Santa Fe assistant, Patricia, who was half-Hispanic and half-Pueblo Indian. Lord, that woman was loud and bright.

"Not so great, lady. I'll be stopping off at my uncle's in Glenwood for the night. Can you push back my appointments tomorrow by an hour? I'll need time to get into Aspen."

"Absolutely. You're not even booked until eleven, and I'll get everyone rescheduled after lunch."

"Thanks. Anything else while I'm stopped?" He might stop at the Golden Burro in Leadville for lunch if they were still open. Maybe Wild Bill's for a burger.

"No, sir. Everything is good here."

"Okay. Well, call me if anything pops up. We'll do online signing if anything has to go tonight."

"Yes, sir. I'm on it."

He didn't doubt that for a second. Eileen only needed him for his signature, and she was better at that than he was. He chuckled. "Thanks, lady. See you tomorrow."

Ford hung up and chewed on his lower lip. He'd go get food, then head to the ranch. His frickin' worst nightmare. The damn place had become his own personal boogeyman, the birthplace of pure cowboy evil.

The thought made him chuckle, shake his head, even as he caught himself grinding his teeth in rage.

There was nothing about his ex, Stoney River, that didn't piss him off, full stop, 100 percent. The guy had made Ford believe they were a thing, hot and heavy, then left him for his ranch and his cousin, for fuck's sake.

A man might be forgiven for never wanting to see that particular face again, right?

Still, if Uncle Ty needed him, he'd go. That was what family did. It had been twelve years, hadn't it? Twelve years was a long time to hold a grudge against a broke-dick liar of a cowboy, and more importantly against the man that had hired said broke-dick liar and given him a place on the ranch that should rightfully have been his.

He'd do what he had to, because Uncle Ty was really the last of his family. At least that he'd ever met. Ford owed the man that much.

He sighed and started the car back up. Time to get a move on. Get this shit over with and move the fuck on.

Story of his whole damned life.

Chapter Two

"STONEY? Stoney, can you please grab those sheets out of the printer?"

Miranda sounded like she was fixin' to tear out her hair, and he was standing right there, so he grabbed them and handed them over before he got his fourth cup of coffee for the day. "You okay, honey? Someone put a burr under your saddle?"

"The Chavez wedding canceled." Miranda sniffled like she might burst into tears.

"The eighty- to ninety-seat guaranteed group?" Fuck a doodle doo. "Jesus. Why?"

"Too far out, weather is looking iffy, her dad, the restaurant owner, wants her to do it there. They're not arguing on me keeping the deposit, but God."

"Yeah." Just what they needed, a huge cancellation in the middle of the summer. If they didn't make their money in the summer and fall, they didn't have another opportunity. They were too far out for either the Sunlight Mountain or Aspen skiers.

"There was a hunting party that wanted that same weekend. I'll call and see if they're still interested."

"Sounds good, lady. Just remember, at this time of year, they can only hunt our private land, not the BLM." God, he didn't want to have to tell Ty. Maybe he just wouldn't mention it. Hell, it wouldn't change a thing one way or the other. Ty had other worries.

"Dad, can I take Lightning out for a ride?" Quartz had slipped in behind him without Stoney even hearing him.

"Not right this second, son. I have to deal with some stuff." He reached over to tousle Quartz's curly hair, but the kid ducked away. "Come on, now. Don't be a pill."

"I'm not! I'll take Bingo with me."

"The dog isn't going to save your butt if you fall off and crack your skull," Stoney said. "Lightning needs more work before he's a pleasure horse, bud."

"I'm bored, Dad. Please. Come on. Isn't there someone who can go out with me?"

"Let me make a couple three phone calls, okay?" Quartz blew out a sigh, but that was the worst symptom of impatience he displayed, so Stoney let it slide. A man had to pick his battles. He grabbed his phone, hunting any cowboy who had an hour to spare his son.

"Sure. Gimme ten." Doogie, who'd been their hunting guide for twenty years, told him. "I'll meet him up to the house."

"I owe you, man." Stoney gave Quartz a grin. "Doogie is going to meet you up to the house and take you. Fair?"

"Yessir." The smile he got in return lit up the whole afternoon. "Thanks, Daddy!"

"No barn until he gets to you, got it?"

"I promise. I do. You rock."

"That's me. Rocking dad." He chuckled. He might have to change the name to the Rocking D someday. He knew better. The ranch was the Leaning N and always would be.

He got a wave, a smile, and then Quartz was gone, boots stamping on the ground.

"Spoiled brat," Stoney said.

"Oh, he is not." Miranda chuckled. "He's such a good boy."

"He is." And God knew Stoney loved him more than life. "Okay, how can I help? What do you need?"

"I don't know?" Her next laugh had an edge of hysteria. "Find more guests."

"Easy. Easy, now. We'll figure it." He didn't bother to bring up the fact that if they didn't get the BLM lease renewed, it wouldn't matter how many guests they had—there would be precious little for them to do.

They had acreage, but the woods, the hunting land.... It was all part of the lease.

"Okay. I—thanks. How's Ty?"

"He's had better days. He's heading back out of town tomorrow."

"Oh, that's a shame." She pulled a face. "I hate that he's so sick."

"We all do." It broke his heart that Ty's kidneys were failing, but shit happened.

"I know. Angie wanted to see you?" She handed him a sticky note. Angie was their stock wrangler.

"I'll head over now. Call me." He slammed back his coffee and jogged to the barn, going to see his favorite dyke.

"Hey!" Angie popped out of a stall, almost giving Stoney a heart attack. "Come see Bella. The new filly."

"Hey, lady. How's she doing?"

"Good! I want you to have a look, though, see what you think of how her conformation looks now."

"Let's do it." He was all over it. He headed into the back where the colts were kept. Bella was their first offspring from a new brood mare, and he had high hopes for this little lady. Dark and fine boned, with a blaze on her forehead—just the sight of her made him grin.

"She's amazing," Angie said, hands on her hips.

"Stunning. And it was an easy delivery too." That was half the battle right there.

"You know it."

Bella lipped at him when he put his hand over the half gate. Gentler than he expected already.

"Hey, Angel Baby. Look at you. Are you gonna grow up to be amazing?" He could handle a couple of good years in the livestock department.

The filly nuzzled his wrist, and Angie laughed. "She's so smart."

"She is. Her momma whispered that I kept carrots hidden away."

"Her momma knows. You spoil Ginblossom like mad."

He shrugged. You had to do something to get the new guys to love you, right? They all responded to some basic love. Hell, that was his basic outlook on life. Don't fuck up. Be nice. Offer carrots.

Stoney grinned. "Anything else? I need to scare up some guests for Miranda."

He fed Bella a carrot, her lips like velvet against his palm. Sweet baby. This was his favorite thing, being out with the animals, doing ranch work.

Hell, sometimes he liked the guests. Well, periodically.

Most of the time, he left them to the employees, but a trail ride now and then was just fine.

"Speaking of guests," Angie said, "do we have any tonight?"

"Not that I know of, honey. Why?"

"Big blue pickup just pulled in. Ty got Sophia coming for supper?"

"Maybe. Stranger things have happened." No. No way. Ty was heading for Grand Junction tomorrow for at least a week, maybe more. "I'll peek in."

"Cool. I mean, I know he told that home health care lady to take a leap." Angie clapped him on the back, damned near sending him stumbling.

"Jesus, woman, you beat your wife that way?" he teased.

"Nope. I'm gentle as a kitten with her. She's tough as nails."

"Remind me to never piss her off."

"Will do, boss. Go check on your uncle." She waved him off, Bella neighing at him when he left.

Stoney saw Quartz out on Lightning, Doogie riding Pink alongside. Doogie would keep the kid in line and make sure he was back in time for supper in about an hour.

God, that was a sight, wasn't it? His cowboy kid. He was passing on a way of life he loved. What more could he ask for?

He didn't know the truck with the New Mexico plates, so he headed into the main house they shared with Ty, curious as all get-out. Late model. Dark blue. A little muddy around the tires. Stoney peered into the windows of the truck. Car charger, leather-bound portfolio. Laptop bag. Locked.

City, then.

Must be a lost guest. He'd go help.

Stoney stomped the dust off his boots and opened the door. The foyer was empty, the door to Ty's half wide open. *Okay. Weird.*

"Uncle Ty? You in here, man?"

"Come on in, Stoney!" Ty called from his study.

Oh. Good. He knew folks were, for the most part, decent, but Ty usually mentioned if company was coming. "Yes, sir. How're you feeling today?"

"Well, I've had better days." Ty smiled at him from behind the desk, looking so normal, which made it that much worse when Stoney turned to smile at Ty's visitor.

Ford Nixel had come home.

Chapter Three

FORD had made it to the ranch an hour before suppertime, which was pretty good, he thought. Gave him a chance to get the lay of the land and talk to Ty before anyone else popped up.

The house…. Jesus, it had changed over the years. Instead of a square frame house, now the old house was the center of two wings, both log-cabin style and stretching out for three windows in either direction. When Ford parked in the old, pitted dirt drive, he didn't know what to do.

He wandered up to the front porch, not sure if he should knock. He settled on calling his uncle, who opened the door before two rings sounded.

Ty waved at him impatiently. When Ford climbed the stairs, Ty grunted. "What are you doing, boy? Get in here."

"Sorry. It's different. You've been working hard."

"Stoney has, you mean. The little son of a bitch is always building something."

"So he's still here, huh?" He knew it, but his steps slowed, because Ford didn't want to see Stoney River, damn it.

"This is his home, Ford. He owns forty-five percent, as you well know."

"I know." He chuckled. "Hope springs eternal." Ford cut anything else right off, because it wasn't fair to Ty. The man loved Stoney like a son, and Ford had chosen to run away from it all those years ago. His bad, not Tyson's. He took a hug, surprised at how skinny Ty felt. "How are you?"

"Dying, but I'm old and that's to be expected."

"You're not that old, man." Tyson was what? Sixty? That was fucking middle-aged these days.

"I am for a Type 2 diabetic who has too much fondness for cinnamon buns and beer." Ty chuckled, whacking him on the back a couple of times. "Come sit with me, kiddo."

Tyson led him into a little office with a huge desk, three cushy chairs, and a half-built Lego Death Star.

How old was the kid now? Nine? Ten? God, how bad was it that he had to think for a minute to come up with Quartz's name? Ford and his cousin, Brittany, had been thick as thieves once. Now she was gone, and Ford's ex was the father of her son....

What the fuck had gone wrong all those years ago?

"Nice office," he told Ty.

"Thank you. I like it. Sit." Tyson eased himself down in his chair with a sigh. "Thank you for coming out, son. I appreciate it."

"I knew it had to be serious for you to ask. What can I do?" He sank down into one of the chairs, the scent of leather and wood oil and horse so strong, so well remembered.

"I'm moving to Grand Junction, Ford. I need dialysis. I got Medicaid now and all, but I need help." Tyson stared at his desk. "I'm not asking you for money, necessarily, but I'm tapped out."

Ford pursed his lips. "Well, if you don't want to take money, what do you want?"

Tyson met his gaze head-on now. "Help with the ranch. Now, Stoney has a good head on his shoulders, but he's a cowboy. We do things the way we've always done them because it's Western, and God knows, we love it, but it ain't working. BLM is fixing to cut off our lease instead of renew it, because our land-use plan is outdated. We can't get the guests with the money to come. I think you're the best hope to keep things going."

Ford blinked, trying to process all that. Tyson didn't want his money outright, which would be a hell of a lot easier.... *Damn.*

"Why me? Surely someone else...."

"Shit, boy. Like I'd screw you out of your half. I wouldn't do that to your daddy. You can buy the five percent and keep the majority vote, or I can lease it to Stoney."

Either way that would give Tyson what he needed to buy a condo in the Junction, or maybe buy a year or two in assisted living. Jesus, his strong-as-an-ox uncle in assisted living. Ford wanted to shout a denial right into Ty's face, but what good would that do?

"Let me think about that for a few days maybe. We'll focus on other things first, like the lease. I'll need the paperwork on that."

"I've got it right here. Stoney's more than capable of dealing with the day-to-day running of the ranch. Shit, the man's a cowboy's cowboy, but… he's no businessman."

"He's not stupid." No, Stoney was a lot of things, and he'd sucked at college-level classes, but Ford knew he was sharp. "What exactly are you trying to do? Improve the ranch, make it less hunting lodge and more guest ranch?"

"I'm trying to retire, Ford." The slow wink was wicked, clever, and made him laugh, just like it was intended to.

"Yeah, yeah, you lazy old fart." Ford grinned. "I mean, that would be my plan, but I have no desire to step on toes." If Brittany's son wasn't in the picture, Ford would just offer to buy out Stoney and turn the ranch into a personal retreat, but that wasn't going to leave any kind of legacy for his…. What? What did he call Quartz? He was a second cousin, but really more like a nephew.

"Stoney wants the world to be like it was in the Old West—where there was land and horses and that was enough. I'm not saying he's hidebound, but he's in love with this place and has been from the first time you brought him."

"Yeah." *Whoa, still bitter much, Ford? Damn.* He forced a smile. "It's good land, but without some new form of income, he'll lose it."

"Yeah, and losing the BLM land is gonna hurt bad. He'll starve before he lets anyone go, and he's the king of second and third and twelfth chances." Ty smiled, the expression fond as hell. "He's a good man, but that doesn't make him a good businessman. I'm protecting him as much as this ranch."

"Well, so long as you know I'm helping out for you and for Quartz, then we're good. I'd let Stoney starve, Ty, and I'm not sorry for it." He had to be upfront.

"That's up to you, Ford. He owns what he owns, and if you go against him, you do." Ty pegged him with a look. "I find out that you speak against him to my grandson, and I will have you skinned alive."

"Hey, I might hold a grudge, but I'm not a solid-gold asshole, Uncle." He wouldn't do that. Especially not the way his mom had badmouthed his dad all these years for having the temerity to die on her.

"Good. Whatever bullshit you two have between you, it's old and you were stupid kids. Let it go and move the fuck on."

"Sure. I'll get right on that." Stung, Ford grabbed the stack of papers on the edge of the desk. "I'll write up a proposal for the BLM."

"Thank you." Tyson waited until their eyes met. "I love you, Ford, as much as if you were mine. You're one hell of a man, and I'm proud."

"Thanks." His ears heated. That meant a lot. "I'm still a work in progress, huh? So you're really leaving tomorrow?"

"I have dialysis. I've been going out there for a few days, coming back in for a day, heading back. It's hard to make the drive, though, and it's confusing to Quartz."

"Have you got a place in mind there?" He would front the money right off if Tyson had a good prospect.

Tyson's cheeks went dark pink. "I have a friend to stay with to begin."

"Like a female-type friend?" he asked. Tyson hadn't dated since Aunt Barbara left him, so far as Ford knew.

"Yep. We'll have lunch sometime soon, all three of us. You'll like her." Tyson chuckled, clearly tickled he'd brazened that out.

"You old dog. Go you, man. Seriously."

"Thanks, son. She works at the hospital, can you believe?" Ty shrugged. "She's offered to come stay here, but Stoney is here, and she'd have to sell her house.... I'd rather go there."

"Sure." That meant no assisted living, right? Ford could get behind that, 100 percent. "Well, if you don't mind, I'll spend the night, kick your ass at cards, and then head into Aspen tomorrow. I'll call the BLM rep in the morning." This was what he did. Land rights, water rights, negotiations. Legal shit. That would be the easy part.

"I appreciate it. Very much. I mean it. I'll have my lawyer draw up papers to transfer the land to you. It'll save you inheritance taxes too."

"Uncle Ty? You in here, man?" The deep voice was immediately recognizable—still pure Texan, still strange from a man of relatively small stature.

"Come on in, Stoney," Ty said, even as Ford shook his head in warning.

"Yes, sir. How are you feeling today?" Stoney asked, and the shock of him walking into the room rendered Ford speechless.

"Well," Ty said. "I've had better days."

Yeah. Better days. So had Stoney, from the look of complete and utter shock on the man's face. Someone hadn't been expecting company.

"But look, Ford is down to visit."

Stoney was still one of the finest men Ford had ever seen—tanned and lean, with a shock of blond hair and eyes the color of a dove's wing. The straw cowboy hat came off, held in gnarled, scarred-up hands. Stoney shot Ford a quick glance, then offered Ty a smile. "I didn't mean to interrupt, sir. I'll get out of your hair. Call if you need me."

"Now, don't run off, son." Ty glanced at Ford, who tried hard not to roll his eyes. "We need to chat too."

"What's up?"

Ford noticed Stoney didn't come any farther into the room, didn't so much as budge.

"I need to tell you about the arrangements I'm making, Stoney. For the ranch and all." Tyson's chin went like a rock, a facial landscape Ford knew all too well. He'd seen it his entire span of teenage years.

Obviously Stoney knew it too, because all vestiges of fidgeting stopped and the man's face went as still as his name. "Lay it on me."

Ty nodded sharply. "I'm going to Grand Junction tomorrow, and I'm gonna stay, at least for the time being. With Sophia."

"Okay. Good deal. She seems like one hell of a lady."

"She is. You're welcome anytime. And of course I'll be around to see Quartz." Ty smiled, a ghost of an expression.

"Well, that's good news. You know he loves you, you old fart."

"I know. I want you two to try to work together."

That had Stoney's eyebrows flying up like Spock's. "Pardon me?"

Ford tried to keep his expression locked down. "How?"

"Stoney, I've signed the ranch over to Ford, my part. You have a new partner. Congratulations."

Stoney River fastened his gaze on Ty, not saying a single word, and not having to. Ty stared back, and then Stoney turned on his heel and left. No stomping, no slamming doors, nothing but pure disgust in the line of the man's shoulders.

"Well," Ford drawled, "that went well."

Shit, way to assure that this situation was going to suck big hairy donkey balls. He didn't give a shit about Stoney, but hell, he didn't need another pain in his ass.

Ty sighed. "I didn't think you'd be here so fast when I called. I was going to talk to him tonight and hope you could make it in tomorrow."

"Nice. What exactly do you want from me, Ty?"

"Fix the BLM lease and make this place something that makes money. Be good to my grandson. Don't kill Stoney."

He could manage the first two. Ford had no idea if the last one was possible.

"Okay, I'll tackle the lease this week. The rest will take some time. I need to look at the operation."

"Of course. Absolutely. Let's talk about the good stuff. How's Santa Fe? I haven't been there in a coon's age."

"Bustling. The tourists are coming in droves." He'd thought a lot about moving his office out toward the rodeo grounds, in fact, getting out of the hectic older part of town near the plaza.

"That's good for the economy, huh? Doesn't help you much, though."

Through the huge window, he saw Stoney head out across the pasture, the man's face like thundercloud. Still, he moved like a man on a mission.

"I do a lot of traveling to the pueblos now instead of people coming to my office." Frankly, all the travel was exhausting, and Ford had been thinking about taking on a partner so he could just stay in one place once in a while. Settle down some.

"Good on you." Ty followed his gaze, smiled. "He'll be fine. He's basically a good guy."

"Honestly, Uncle Ty, I don't give a shit. You sure it's okay for me to spend the night?"

"Of course. We'll have potato soup and bread. Rumor is that there's sweet potato pie too."

"Yum. Okay. I'm gonna go grab some stuff out of my truck, maybe move it around by the old barn." He would talk to Ty again this evening, try to pry more details out of him.

"That works. Don't block the silver duallie."

"You got it." He rose, then bent to give Ty a brief hug. This man had raised him as much as anyone had, and Ty was sick now. It broke Ford's heart a little.

"You can stay over on this side. It's the room with the big wooden four-poster."

"Got it. I'll see you at supper, old man." Ford kept it light. The shit would hit the fan soon enough.

"Yessir. Take it easy."

Ford headed out to his truck to grab his bags so he could get a little work in at least.

He felt eyes on him from every angle. He swore he could sense Stoney's fury, focused on him like a laser.

Good. Good. Let the fucker burn with it. They'd both need a healthy dose of rage to make it through this. Ford grabbed his laptop case and his rollaboard, breathing deep. Glenwood had a unique smell, all woodsmoke and green, mountain and canyon mixed.

Magic.

This place was magic, and Stoney River had stolen it from him.

Ford blinked away the moisture trying to rise in his eyes. Anger or sadness, it didn't matter. Never let them see you sweat, even from the eyes.

Eye sweat.

For fuck's sake.

He was losing his mind. Obviously he was dehydrated. Leadville did that to a man. Even someone who lived at 7000 feet all year long.

"Daddy! Daddy, we ran! Did you see?"

"I saw, son. Very good. You walk him out now, okay?" Stoney's voice was calm, warm, and surprised the heck out of Ford, wherever the hell he was.

"Okay. Just a sip of water, right?"

"Yes, son. Good memory. Doogie, you got this, man? I got to…."

"Go on, boss. Me and Quartz can keep each other busy for a week."

"I'll buy you a beer tonight, buddy."

"Whenever you get the chance." Doogie had that old cowboy look, the kind that told Ford he'd been around the block more than once. Hell, Doogie had been around the block more than once before Ford had left all those years ago.

"You mind Doogie, boy."

"Yessir!" That was a happy kid.

God. Brittany and Ford had been close once upon a time, and he wanted her son happy. He did.

He headed back into the house, trying not to dread... well, everything about the next few hours. That was impossible, so yeah, Ford just needed to suck it up. He pulled out his phone, knowing Eileen would still be at the office.

"Good afternoon, sir. How's it going?"

"I think I went to Hell and not Glenwood. I need to set a meeting with whoever is doing the BLM leasing in my uncle's quadrant. ASAP."

He could hear her typing, the sound furious on the keyboard. "ASAP as in tomorrow?"

"If possible. If not, we'll go Monday. One way or the other, I'll have a proposal ready." That would be his first real act as owner, right?

"I'm on it. Anything else?"

"I need to know if Quartz River goes to school locally." Something told him the kid was homeschooled, but he wanted to know the situation for sure.

"Quartz like the rock?"

"Yes, ma'am. My nephew. Well, technically, he's my cousin Brittany's kid." He knew nothing about Quartz, really, and suddenly he was ashamed of that fact.

"I'll have all the pertinent information forwarded ASAP, sir."

"Thanks. Lunch on me tomorrow."

"Those are my favorite words, you know."

"I do." She would make him take her to Creperie du Village or something froufy like that. Eileen had an unnatural fondness for fondue.

Of course, interactive food made him happy, so he'd take it.

"Thanks, lady. See you tomorrow." He opened his laptop once he got to his room, and immediately had to go hunting Ty again. "Hey! Is there Wi-Fi?"

"There is. The password changes every day. Wait. I think that's just for guests. Hold on." Ty grabbed his phone. "Miranda honey, what do we do for Wi-Fi here? Ah. Ah, right. Thanks. Use the notforpublicconsumption deal and the password is stoneysaysso."

"Stoney…. Right." *Grr*. Ford shook his head. Lord. He had to get over this whole thing where Stoney's name made him grit his teeth.

"Y'all can talk about changing it. I just put it in the once and it's saved."

"No problem." He turned on his heel, heading back to his room. Hiding.

Fuck.

Fuck a doodle doo.

What was he supposed to do now?

Chapter Four

STONEY saddled up Button and headed up into the trees, barely holding his shit together. What had Ty been thinking? Ford Nixel hated him with the passion of a thousand fiery suns, and Ty knew that. Ty knew that.

Why on earth would he call Ford in without telling Stoney? Without any warning? They'd talked about how sick Ty was or wasn't a hundred times. Stoney could handle this.

Hell, he knew Ford was going to inherit his part, but he…. He what?

Was going to buy Ford out?

Like he'd ever be able to afford that.

He'd just been hoping like hell he'd have a better plan than work his ass off and still not get anywhere.

Stoney had been putting off making any improvements to the guest areas until he got the lease renewed, but Aaron Harris over at the BLM had been putting him off for weeks. He was just going down in flames.

This was…. God help him, living on this ranch was one of the few things he'd done right in his life. Living and working the ranch and raising Quartz. Folks didn't understand that. That he was doing the only things he knew how to do.

Button danced, and Stoney realized he was communicating his worry to her, that he was making her nervous with his bad energy. Horses were so sensitive to that shit.

"Sorry. Sorry. Let's just run, baby girl. Let's go." They wouldn't run, of course, the terrain was too wild, too unstable, and he wouldn't risk her for love or money, much less for a fucking temper tantrum.

Still, Stoney gave her all the rein she needed to take her head, and she took off at a gentle canter. That would work, get them both out of their moods.

How the hell was he going to manage this? To work with Ford? To… to forgive Ty for not at least talking to him first, like he was just some employee, some manager.

This was his home, right?

God, what if Ford tried to get rid of him and Quartz? He couldn't make them go legally, but he could make it awful for them. Forty-five percent. That was what he owned.

Forty-five percent and Ty had done that on purpose, he guessed, so Stoney didn't have the chance to be an equal partner, and he got that, he did. He wasn't really family; he wasn't really anything but a broke-dick cowboy working a hunting lodge.

"God *damn* it!" he yelled, the birds flying up out of the trees. Great, now he was scaring the wildlife. If he didn't need to be there for Quartz, he could just pray for a bear attack.

Stoney started laughing, the sound not the least bit happy. He'd come up here, and he'd known, from the second he'd stepped foot on the Leaning N, that this was the answer to his problems, this was his way out of the mess he was.

He'd sacrificed what little he had left to stay too. He'd sacrificed whatever he might have been building with Ford. College had been a loss for him, so that hadn't been hard to give up, but Ford—

Well, an up-and-comer like Ford would never have stayed with a loser like him. A loser who was failing out of UNM, who was living on ramen and saltines while Ford was driving a brand-new car, eating out every day, and rocking his 4.0.

God, the son of a bitch had been a wet dream come to life. Dark headed with the deepest green eyes Stoney had ever seen, and, Christ almighty, Ford had been so sensual, so out there, coming on to him and turning him inside out. Stoney had been stupid for the fine motherfucker.

Ford had seemed pretty over the moon for Stoney too, but now he wondered…. If it had been that easy to just dump his ass, it must have been sex alone.

Hell, they'd been kids. Twenty-year-old kids from opposite sides of the universe. Maybe they'd both been idiots and all these years were more about the ranch than anything…. Oh, fuck, he could ponder the reasons forever, and it wouldn't matter.

Ford Nixel hated his guts.

Not only that, but Ford had control of the ranch and the future of Stoney's little boy.

He closed his eyes. Okay. Okay, it was damned near suppertime, and he needed to get back, go have dinner like a civilized, polite feller. Quartz needed him to play the game.

Maybe he could just keep Quartz in and they could have peanut butter and banana sandwiches in front of the TV.

Then again, his kid would never forgive him for not letting him in on anything new and different at the ranch, including an older second cousin he'd never met. Ford had sent flowers to Brit's funeral, but that was it.

"Shit, Brittany. What the fuck am I going to do?" He chuckled as he asked the question, because Brit had been the least capable human being on earth. She'd loved the river, and that was it. Not even Quartz had changed that fact, no matter how much everyone had expected it to. She was an addict. If it was about rafting or kayaking, she could do it. Ranch work, well, not so much.

At least she died doing what she loved, he guessed.

Oh, who the fuck was he kidding? She was supposed to be here helping take care of her son. Loving Quartz. Stoney adored the boy, but Quartz could have used a woman's influence.

Maybe that's what Ford could do.

God, he cracked himself right the fuck up. He nudged Button back toward the house, his belly rumbling. Hunger was finally going to be what beat him down. Sad state of affairs.

He walked out his mount when he got back to the barn, just like he'd told Quartz to do. Lead by example, Ty had always told him. Stoney wondered what Ty meant to show him by way of example with this latest stunt.

Maybe that he wasn't worth trusting without Ty there.

Stoney sighed. That wasn't fair. Ty had been away more than he'd been at the ranch for two years. Maybe he was sicker than Stoney knew. Scared. Whatever. The only thing Stoney had to his name was this ranch, and he had a son to support.

He didn't have the luxury of pride.

He put Button up after a few sips of water and a handful of feed, then went to wash up. Geoff would serve up supper soon.

"Daddy! Daddy, you went for a long ride. Were you mad?" His boy might not be the most agile socially, but he paid attention.

"Just stressed out and needing to let it go. Put myself in time out."

Quartz nodded. "I drew a roller coaster to build."

"Did you? Show me." He loved his kid's drawings. Quartz designed these amazing flights of fancy.

He sat in his chair, tugging his work boots off while Quartz went to fetch his drawings from the kitchen table. "Look! See? It has a loop and a big dip."

"Dude, that would make folks scream like idiots, wouldn't it?"

"Not you, Daddy."

"No sir. Not me." He didn't lose his shit in front of anyone. Not under any circumstance.

"See? My daddy is brave." Quartz glanced at him from under his lashes. "Who's here to see Grandpa?"

"Your second cousin, Ford. He is your momma's cousin."

"Oh. I've never met him." Quartz watched him, waiting to see if he should be upset or happy.

"No, you haven't. He looks a lot like your momma. He's a lawyer. He lives in Santa Fe."

"That's in New Mexico. Are we going to supper?"

"It is and we are. Let me get cleaned up right quick, okay, son?" God, he didn't want to go. He wanted to stay in here and watch *NCIS* and have a stiff drink.

"I'm hungry, Daddy."

"I know. I get it. Let me grab a clean shirt. Get my going-to-supper boots?"

"Yessir." Quartz ran off and grabbed his boots.

Stoney pulled on a fresh shirt and tucked it in.

Lord, help him make it through supper without saying a word. Well, at least not a bad word. He didn't talk at all, Quartz would know something was wrong.

Maybe he could stick with "pass the salt," "another roll please," and "kiss my ass, you motherfucker."

Oh wait. That last one would be bad.

He chuckled at the thought, though, didn't he? Stoney liked it.

He tugged on his boots before they headed to the big communal dining area. They ate out here nine nights out of ten, all of them a family.

His mouth tugged down. Ty was leaving them.

"Daddy?"

"What, son?"

"It's dinnertime."

"I know, buddy. We're here, right?" Though no one else was. Huh.

"Uh-huh. Where's Grandpa?"

"I don't know. Why don't you see if Geoff needs help?" He would go hunt down the assholes who were disappointing his son. With a club.

He grabbed his phone and texted Ty. "Where y'at?"

"On my way. Was in the storeroom with Ford."

Ty could text like a fiend.

"K." Next he texted Angie "Git here with the crew. Do NOT leave me to this or ur dead."

"On it, bud," she sent back.

His phone chimed twice more—Doogie and Geoff checking in. Yeah. His team loved him.

He found the chair in the corner and closest to the door. He was out of here as soon as he could do it without pissing off Ty.

Miranda showed up first, grinning and winking. "I made it. Anything I shouldn't be talking about?"

"Just let me get out of speaking and I'll be happy. I just want to sit and eat." He wanted to tell her that Ty had sold out, but that wasn't his tale to tell.

"Okay."

Angie came trotting in, eyes bright with curiosity. "So is that really Ty's nephew?"

"He is. Lawyer from Santa Fe. Older than Brittany. My age."

"Huh. Baggage." Angie studied him, nodding when he just stared back. "Lots."

"Tons. Twelve years' worth."

"Ouch." She knew him, knew his history.

"Twelve what, Daddy?" Quartz wandered in carrying plates and bowls. "Geoff says family-style tonight."

"Does he need help, son?"

"Way to deflect," Angie muttered.

He wanted to kick her, but she was saved when Ty walked in with Doogie and Ford.

"Quartz found us and informed us he was hungry," Ty said, and Stoney answered with a half smile. Quartz wasn't shy about letting folks know what he needed.

"Good thing too," Ford murmured. "Ty was getting puny."

"Sit, huh. You let us fetch and carry." He stood and helped Ty to a chair. "Stubborn old fuck. You're wearing yourself out."

"I'm fine." Ty gave him a mutinous look but then grinned at Quartz. "This is your momma's cousin, Ford."

Quartz gave Ford a long look. "You live in New Mexico."

"I do. I also have an office in Aspen." Ford nodded easily, not really smiling, but not being ugly. "Nice to meet you, Quartz."

"Nice to meet you." Quartz nodded, the motion so adult, so firm. "I'm going to go help Geoff with the soup."

"Thanks, kiddo. Geoff can always use a hand." He praised, because Quartz wasn't melting down, was focused and helpful.

Quartz nodded and hustled out while Ty did the introductions. Stoney moved back to his chair in the shadows where he could watch without being seen.

Ford looked damn good. No lines around his eyes, hair dark and sleek as a raven's wing, classy as fuck. Of course he did. He'd always been meant for fine things, that Ford.

Quartz brought the bread in, holding it carefully, and Geoff brought the tureen. Every single time Stoney saw the hipster, lumberjack chic, metrosexual, yoga guru, vegetarian chef he smiled. Every time.

Crazy fucker.

Ford stared a little, and yeah, surprise! Stoney loved that shocked look. He shouldn't be a jerk, but he had to stifle a laugh. Geoff was a force to be reckoned with, and the man had a huge heart.

A crazy brain, but a huge heart.

Geoff beamed at all of them. "Gang's all here, huh? Hi, I'm Geoff. You must be Ford. Ty says you're a busy guy. Thanks for coming."

Ford blinked at him, then held out one hand. "Pleased."

"Let me put down the soup, and I'll get a hug. I'm a hugger."

Ford took on the expression of a pit bull being lifted onto a vet table. Pure *God no*.

Oh, that was too fucking funny.

Geoff put the tureen on the table and grabbed Ford. Geoff didn't give man hugs. Oh no. This was full-on, holding tight and being in touch with your personal feelings embracing.

It couldn't happen to a nicer guy.

Stiff as a board, Ford patted Geoff's back. "Uh. Thanks."

"Nice to meet you, man. Let's eat!" Geoff served with Quartz, humming softly, smiling at everyone but Ford.

"This is Angie and Miranda," Ty said when he settled, grabbing his napkin.

"I'm head of sales and marketing, and Miss Angie is…." Mira trailed off.

"Just a wrangler and just Angie."

"Good to meet you both." Ford glanced at Stoney, lips tightening, "Stoney."

"Mmhmm." Ford was well aware of who he was.

"Well, this is cozy." Geoff plopped down, drawing Ford's attention. "Lawyer, huh?"

"I am, yes. I do mostly Native American land and water rights."

"Yeah? Rock on, dude. That's important sh… stuff. That's honorable work. You live close by?"

"Santa Fe."

Yeah, Ford didn't mention he lived part of the year in Aspen but he'd never met Quartz. Not that Stoney was bitter.

To be honest, it was best that Ford stayed away from his son. The man was trouble.

Okay, Ford wasn't trouble, but Stoney still didn't want him here.

"Nice." Geoff chuckled. "I worked at the Plaza Café for six weeks."

Seriously? Had Geoff worked everywhere on earth? He'd never heard the man not say, "I worked at Whatever Random Restaurant for Some Tiny Amount of Time."

"Traveler, huh?" Ford relaxed some, nodding and smiling. "Where was your favorite job?"

"I love it here, but the best job ever was at a little joint called Hank's in Monterey. Impossible to afford a place there, though."

"God, yeah." Ford laughed. "The sea lions are cool."

"And the fog. I loved the fog." Geoff bounced. "You're familiar with the area, I take it."

"I love Monterey. I did a case there over military encroachment. I wasn't popular."

Ford kept talking, and Stoney stopped listening, eating his soup and trying to focus on tomorrow's list. He wanted to move the cattle down into the low pasture, and he needed to figure out whether he should grade the driveway now or just wait for spring.

"Right, Stoney?" Ty was glaring at him.

"Hmm?" Oh, for fuck's sake. Why did Ty insist on humiliating him?

"That wedding canceled, right? Can we get those hunters to commit to November?"

"The wedding did cancel. I'm working on the hunters from Texas, yes." That wasn't his motherfucking job; it was Mira's.

Mira stammered at Ty. "Assuming, of course, the lease—"

"I have a meeting with the BLM rep tomorrow in Aspen." Ford waved a hand. "Get the hunters scheduled."

The staff all blinked, then looked to Stoney as if they were one person. *Damn.* "We'll chat, Mira. No worries."

He kept his voice calm, easy. No way he was letting anyone know how mad he was.

"Okay." She nodded and broke off a piece of bread. "This is great, Geoff."

When he glanced at Ford, the man was staring intently at him, fairly emotionless. He raised an eyebrow, and then he let himself smile, cool as he could.

Ford snorted audibly, which had Angie offering him a red bandana. "Nose problems?"

Oh, that was his Ang. That woman had his back.

"Daddy, is your soup good?"

"Huh? It is, yes." He took a bite, but it tasted like dust.

"I chopped. Before I went out with Doogie. I like cheffing."

"Did you? Excellent. I like the onions."

"Thank you!" The littlest bit of praise made his kid beam.

Geoff nodded easily. "He's a champ."

"He is." Stoney winked at Geoff. "You'll have him making Thanksgiving supper in no time."

"You know it. My celery buddy."

"I like celery with peanut butter."

"I like it with pimento cheese," Stoney countered.

"I like it with squeezy cheese," Angie said, and Quartz groaned.

"Ewww."

He leaned close, whispered softly. "Squee-ee-eezy cheese."

Quartz made more ick noises, but Ford chuckled warmly. "Bacon squeezy cheese."

Stoney shot Ford a quick look, and damn if he didn't almost smile. Fucker.

"Oh, God. On Triscuits," Angie murmured. "You and me, Mr. Nephew. Midnight."

"You're on."

Stoney did chuckle this time, and then he pushed his chair back and picked up his bowl. "I hope y'all can excuse me. I'm having a bit of a cramp."

"Are you done, Daddy? I'll go with you." Quartz was done. Stoney could see it on his son's little face.

"I am. Tell your grandpa good night."

"There's sweet potato pie. Take some for later when you both feel better," Geoff said, giving him a knowing look full of sympathy.

"Thanks, man. I appreciate it." He cut two good-sized pieces. "Night, y'all."

"Night, Grandpa." Quartz pecked Ty's cheek. Then he bobbed his head at Ford. "Night."

"Good night, Quartz." Ford's tone was genuinely kind.

"Good night. Come on, Daddy. We need our quiet time together."

Yes. Yes, they did. They watched silly TV and ate dessert together and did Quartz's schoolwork. By the time that he got his happy ass to bed with a stiff drink in hand, he was almost not pondering homicide.

Almost.

Chapter Five

FORD had debated long and hard about wearing the tie.

In the end, he left it off. He actually remembered Mr. Beacon from his high school years. The man was a BLM manager now, but he'd been a conservation guy back in Ford's day, visiting schools with the Colorado State extension service.

He wasn't a formal type, and the tie would set the wrong tone. Ford went with a button-down shirt with subtle Western styling and gray dress pants over cowboy boots.

His good felt hat completed the look, and damn, he looked good if he did say so himself. People he knew now teased him about being a Coca-Cola cowboy, but he had grown up on a ranch, after all. He could go rodeo any day.

Mr. Beacon met him at the door, wrinkled face wreathed in a smile. "Ford Nixel! I'll be damned!"

"Mr. Beacon. How are you, sir?" He shook hands, feeling better already.

"I'm good. Good. Come on in and have a seat. Get yourself a cup of coffee. I know Aaron Harris was handling this with Ty, but I wanted to hear the new plans when I got your petition."

"Thank you." Beacon had one of those cup-by-cup makers, so Ford popped in a caramel latte cup and ran water through. "Wow, so how long have you been here?"

"Six years? Seven? It's a good job. I feel like it's a good place to retire. What are you up to these days?"

"Mineral and water rights mostly. I have an office down in Santa Fe." He didn't mention Aspen.

"Nice. I like it down there. Some neat architecture."

"I work a lot on the Four Corners reservation areas and the Pueblos." He loved helping the different tribes keep control of what little they'd been able to carve out for themselves.

"Good on you. Public service is fulfilling as hell." Beacon leaned back, shot him a look. "So, why are you in my office instead of Stoney?"

"The lease is coming up at the Leaning N. I know it's been tough for Ty and Stoney the last few years, but they did manage to solicit a good many of the public comments and get you the references they need."

"Yeah. Yeah, I hate that Tyson is so ill and leaving the ranch. That's been Nixel land for generations."

"I know." Ford paused to gather his thoughts. "Stoney is a good manager, but I feel as though the land-use plan needs a review. I have some ideas."

Beacon's eyebrow went up. "So, you did do the petition. You're coming back home?"

"Well, I'm going to be spending a good bit of time here. I'll have to go to Santa Fe at least a week a month, but I've promised Ty I would help out."

"That's good news. It's good to have a local there."

Because even after more than ten years, Stoney was still just a Texan. Coloradans often said if Texans would just go home, they'd gain a thousand feet in elevation....

"I hope so." Ford had no intention of living at the ranch, did he? "At any rate, I don't intend to change the grazing lease, but the hunting and forest permits I have some great thoughts about."

"Well, I'm willing to cut you some slack, since Ty's so ill, but we're coming on short days, so we need some movement."

"We do." He nodded decisively, taking a deep breath before he launched into his well-ordered spiel. He'd surprised himself with the idea that had popped into his head last night.

At the end, Beacon was leaning back and grinning. "No shit? Well, it's unique and, I got to tell you, timely."

"That's what I thought. Aspen has always been progressive, and Glenwood has the hot springs. I think it will be a draw."

"I assume this is all in the paperwork I got?"

"I have an initial proposal. I can have a notarized application to you by the end of business today." Ford almost held his breath. No approval would come for at least a month. There were hoops to jump through, but it sounded as if Beacon didn't intend to put him at the end of the line.

"Good deal. Ty's a good man, respected around here."

"Yessir." He wanted to ask what Beacon thought of Stoney, but he was pretty sure the omission told him something. To be fair, he would bet a lot of folks knew Stoney by name only.

If nothing else, Stoney was just Quartz's daddy, and it was pretty obvious the boy adored his dad. He sighed. Ford thought of himself as a fair man. Automatically thinking ill of Stoney didn't suit him.

Still, he was tender on the edges, and who could blame him? Thrown over for his family and his family's land? Ford still had more than his share of rage.

"I think you may have a workable plan, Ford. We can possibly make this work."

"That's great news." He stood when Beacon did. "Thank you."

"Get that paperwork over here, and we'll make things move."

"I will. Thank you." He shook hands one more time before Beacon walked him to the door.

"Holler when you're ready, and we'll grab lunch." Beacon nodded and smiled.

Ford headed out. Okay. Meeting one, down. Check.

Ty was going to be pleased as hell, and Ford couldn't help but feel smug. He allowed himself a grin on the way out to the truck.

There was nothing like being superefficient to make a man feel ten feet tall.

Now he just needed to get the rest of his shit finished so he could go have a steak.

Chapter Six

STONEY got Quartz to Miss Alanna's room, grabbed his insulated coffee cup, and headed to the office. Maybe he could get the contact number of those hunters and get them out here with a private hunting guide.

Yeah. Okay, he could put together an attractive package, get with Geoff on a good menu for rustic but elegant.

Elegant.

He snorted at himself. Did that mean Chinet instead of generic paper plates?

"Morning," Ty said when Stoney walked into the office. "Nippy out there today for so early in the year."

"Yes, sir. Gon' be winter before we know it." He couldn't hardly look at Ty.

"Sit down, son." Ty's voice had a little iron in it. "We need to talk."

"Surely." He kept his voice calm, kept himself from saying what the fuck are you doing?

He sat, knowing Ty had his reasons, even if that didn't make it a bit easier. Ty always had an angle. Him? He was sorta round in his soul. Nothing bumped off him.

Ty sighed, turning in his chair to face Stoney. "I know I should have told you."

"It's your right to do as you want."

Ty should have said something. Stoney had been managing this land for a decade, he'd raised Quartz, and he'd done every single fucking thing Ty had asked of him, without question.

Ty didn't fucking trust him to….

Breathe. Just breathe.

"I was going to go to Grand Junction and leave it to you, Stoney. I was. But Harris kept not returning my calls, and that feller from the tax office kept calling, and I knew." Ty shook his head, spreading his hands. "We needed someone like Ford."

His cheeks flooded with heat, the shame almost too much to bear, and he swallowed around the ball that formed in his throat. "Yes, sir."

Stoney couldn't believe this. He couldn't even start to wrap his mind around it. He'd thought…. Hell, he'd thought he was good at this. He'd really thought he was doing a good job—at being a good man, one hell of a cowboy, a decent dad.

Nothing like having one of them rugs yanked free to show the filth beneath.

Ty gave him a sharp look. "Now, you stop that. Got nothing to do with you." Yeah, Ty always said he wore his every thought on his face.

"No, sir." *What the fuck does it have to do with, then?*

"I'm sick, Stoney. Real sick." Ty's face crumpled. "I'm sorry, kiddo."

"No worries. You just focus on getting better and taking care of that lady of yours." He wasn't getting into this with Ty. No way. Ty made his decisions for his reasons, and if Stoney was disappointed, that wasn't none of Ty's. "You coming to move your stuff soon? This isn't it, right?"

He needed time to prepare his son.

"I'll be back in about three days. I have a treatment tomorrow, and that will leave me puny."

Yeah, the drop in blood pressure made Ty feel like hammered shit.

"Good deal. You be careful on your drive." Stoney stood and held one hand out to Ty. "Have a good one."

Ty studied him for a long moment, then shook with him. "Okay. I'll call when I get in."

"Call Quartz at bedtime, please. He counts on hearing your voice." He needed a fucking cigarette, and he'd bet Angie and him could sneak one in the old barn.

"I will. I swear." Ty hugged him, not letting him avoid it.

He patted Ty's back, letting the casual smile fall from his face. He was going to let Ty have the office until he left, but Ty had been waiting for him, clearly, because he muscled past Stoney. "I'll go on and get out of your hair."

"Have a good one." He waited for Ty to disappear, then texted Angie.

Smoke?
Meet you at the colt barn
K

Thank God.

He got his laptop turned on before heading out. It was so old it took forever to boot up. He could smoke a pack and come back to it.

Okay, he wouldn't have a whole pack, but, damn, he wanted to.

He jogged out to the barn, searching for Angie.

"Psst. Geoff is out talking to the goats. Come on."

"Oh, God." Geoff would lecture them forever if he caught them. "I know, right? Last thing I need today is a lecture." He was holding on to his temper with both hands.

"I get that." She gave him a sympathetic smile. "Regular or menthol?"

"You have both?" Impressive.

"I couldn't gauge your mood, and Doogie likes menthol with his coffee and Bailey's."

"Works for me, lady. Christ, I have a headache."

"Well, make this one good, then. One smoke is enough."

He lit up and took a deep draw. God, he wanted to throw his head back and scream. The cigarette smoke burned hard enough to satisfy the urge.

"You gonna tell me what's up, boss?"

"Ty turned over his part of the ranch to Ford."

Angie blinked. "The lawyer?"

"Yes, ma'am."

"Why?" She waved the hand holding her cigarette. "Sorry. I mean, I know Ty is sick."

"He said that he needed someone here who can run things better."

"Oh. Oh, no. Are you not going to be the boss?"

"I own forty-five percent. He can't fire me, can he?"

"No." Her mouth firmed. "We'll walk out."

"So, I'll be the boss until they drag me out kicking and screaming. It's not like he's going to be here, for God's sake." Right? Ford wouldn't live out in the sticks. He'd been in Aspen, at the closest. Let him renegotiate the lease and shit. Then Ford would leave.

He'd raise Quartz up and then figure out what to do from there. That would be a few short years, the way the kid was growing like a weed.

He took another drag, his mind going a million miles a minute.

"So, what's Ty going to do?"

"Moving to Grand Junction with his new lady."

"Well, that will put him close to his doctors." She chewed her lip. "Damn, Stoney."

"Yeah. I know. Ford hates me." Stoney couldn't even blame the man.

"Why?" She blinked at him owlishly. She had to know some of the story, people talked, but Stoney tried not to think about Ford.

"We dated at UNM. He was... shit. I was a hick from Nowhere, Texas, and he was this out, sexual dude. We went together for two, two and a half years." Then Stoney had failed out of college, and before he'd told Ford the truth, he'd come to the Leaning N and Ty offered him a job.

That was the big blowup, and he'd never had another chance to explain. Ford had gone on to grad school, and he'd grown roots in Colorado.

Then Brit and Ty had come to him, asked him to stand up as Quartz's daddy, and he had a son and a home and a life better than any he was going to get otherwise.

Stoney wouldn't do anything different now, except for telling Ford the truth back then. He'd had too much pride to admit he just wasn't good enough, wasn't smart enough to run with the big dogs. He still couldn't.

This was his speed.

Angie gave him a one-armed hug. "I adore you, bud."

"You know, if either one of us was straight and your wife wouldn't kill me, I'd make you happy."

She chortled. "I know! She would brain you with a skillet."

"She'd tear my heart out with her bare teeth."

"I'm glad you respect her as she deserves," Angie said.

"You know I adore her." Hetty was a stud.

"I do."

He stubbed out his smoke. "I need to work in the office."

"Yuck. You want to ride out this afternoon? Check fence?"

Like they needed to ride fence. Still, by then he would need fresh air and freedom. "I do. Holler at me after lunch."

"I can do that. Chin up, boss. We got your back. Ain't no one going to mess up things for you and Quartz."

"Thank you, ma'am."

She waved him off, and Stoney figured he was getting old. One cigarette and he was all scratchy in the throat.

Still, maybe he could get those hunters out here and make them all some money.

It was worth a try.

Chapter Seven

FORD held a notebook and his iPhone, taking pictures and making notes. The barns were in good repair, the main house an extravaganza waiting to happen. What needed all the work were the outbuildings that seemed suitable for Ford's plan: the old bunkhouse, two large storage sheds, and then five or six guest cabins mostly used by hunters.

He could put in more cabins, maybe a pretty outdoor space for some events….

This place could be a showpiece. A prize, for fuck's sake. The scenery was pristine, the views amazing, and damn it, he was going to make this work.

A gay-friendly meeting place, a rustic resort and event destination.

Ford glanced around, hoping his gleeful laugh didn't sound nuts.

The woman who seemed to run the livestock and be Stoney's second-in-command met his gaze, one eyebrow lifted.

Ford winked. "Good ideas make me happy." Might as well start out like he could hold out.

"Good for you. You need something?"

"I'm just getting a feel for the improvements since I was here last." Did she know he owned half the ranch? She was snappy.

"I've been here for eight years. You got questions, holler."

The words were straightforward and probably not as acrimonious as Ford took them to be, so he kept his shoulders down, nodding easily. "Thanks. Are you the wrangler?"

"Yes, sir. Me and Stoney met at a rodeo event. I was riding safety, and he was impressed."

"No shit? How did the guys know where to grab you?" He chuckled, hoping she took him like he meant it. Rodeo men could be downright terrified of a female in the arena.

"As butch as I am, I just wrapped my boobs. It made it easier."

"There you go." Ford pondered his notes. "How many guest horses do we have trained for trails and such right now?"

"Eleven. We've got a few that are trainable that we would ride, our personal mounts, and the packhorses."

"What about the herd I saw on the way in? There were about twenty."

Angie nodded. "Stoney's mustang project. It's in the land-use information."

"I'll look it up. Stoney chooses the stock, or do you?"

"We do it together. We know horse flesh, and my wife is a breeder."

Man, she was leaving herself wide open for all sorts of bitchy gay jokes, but Ford pushed the words down. This wasn't Santa Gay, and she didn't deserve his growly.

Her dark gaze landed on him as heavy as a boulder, and he'd be damned if he didn't feel like she was reading his mind.

"What's her specialty?" Ford finally asked. "Quarter horses?"

"Belgians."

Jesus. Those things were huge. Pullers, those beasts, and popular in Colorado, thanks to the Coors hitch. That could be a tourist draw.

"Does she compete with them?"

"Sometimes. Mostly she runs a breeding operation, but she has a four—and a six-hitch."

"Nice." Ford liked Angie a lot already. She was loaded for bear on not liking him, he could tell, but they'd do all right. God knew what Stoney had told her about him.

Obviously Stoney didn't have a problem hiring the L in the rainbow. Hell, he guessed Stoney swung all ways. He'd had no problem giving it up for Ford, then turning around and giving it to Brittany. His mouth tightened. "Anything else I should know about the horse operation?"

"What's to know? The yearlings are gorgeous. We have a three-year-old that's coming into her own. We're not interacting with the mustangs unless they need medical care."

"All good to know." The mustangs needed to be moved to a higher pasture, then. They could survive harder winter conditions, and more guests meant too much interaction.

The sound of Garth singing about rodeo sounded, and Angie grabbed her phone. "Excuse me. Hey, baby. Yeah? No, I'm gonna be home for supper tonight. Pizza's fine."

Pizza sounded amazing, in fact. Huh. Maybe Ford would run in to…. Damn. Beau Jo's had closed in Glenwood. So had Marshall Dillon's, which he'd loved as a kid.

No fucking fair. Maybe that Geoff kid could make a good crust.

He waited for Angie, because it was polite, lifting a hand when she hung up. "Thanks for letting me pick your brain."

"No worries. Have a good one, man."

Ford nodded and headed for the kitchen at the main house, the idea of a thick crust mountain-ish pie a sudden obsession.

The big kitchen was in the back with its own door so no one had to interrupt either Ty or Stoney. That also allowed access to the grill and the smoker, and a separate fire exit as well. Smart design.

The place had changed, that was for sure, and he had to admire Ty for that. It was easy to let things stagnate. For all he knew, Stoney was the one behind it, but Ty could easily have dug in and said no.

Something amazing hit his nose when he walked into the kitchen, strong and spicy. Indian food, maybe.

Geoff was dancing, rocking back and forth, singing at the top of his lungs. Now, Ford had no idea what Geoff was singing—Tibetan throat songs, maybe.

When Geoff saw Ford, he winked, then hit the big finale note. Boom. Oh, very nice.

Ford applauded, and Geoff took a bow.

"Thank you. I'm here all day. What's up, new bossman?"

"I want a pizza. A thick, cheesy, amazing pizza."

"Hmm." Geoff put his hands on his hips and looked Ford over. "Chicago thick? Sicilian?"

"Colorado mountain pie."

"Ahhhh." Geoff rolled his eyes and smacked his lips before walking to the pantry so he could tug out flour and yeast, sugar and honey. "I see where we're going. What do you like on?"

"Yes. I like it all." Pepperoni, sausage, hamburger, onions, peppers, olives—all of it.

"Coolios. Side dishes? I can't really justify the salad bar in the bathtub, but I do have a wicked selection of pickled veg."

Geoff was kind of a hoot.

"Just feed me something that is better than sex, man."

Geoff pulled a face. "Food is always better than sex, because food doesn't let you down if you prep well."

"Man, that's deep." And sad.

"Mmm. I have hidden layers. I had a chef in France tell me I loved like an artichoke. A leaf for many, a heart for one. He just wasn't it."

"I'm more like a—"

"Pineapple." Stoney walked through, grabbed a sandwich from a platter, and kept going. "The smell ain't bad, and he's juicy enough, but you sure don't want him near your tender bits when he's mad."

Then the little son of a bitch kept walking.

Geoff burst out laughing, the sound bouncing off the walls.

Ford had to grin. "Man, he didn't leave me any opportunity for a comeback, did he?"

"That's not how he zings—he walks in, drops a bomb, then walks out."

"Huh. He used to be scared to engage at all."

"I'd say disinterested more than scared. I've seen him stare down a pack of armed guys without so much as a blink."

"What? When?" Alarmed, he turned to stare at Geoff.

"He guides hunters. You don't think they can get aggressive when they don't get what they want?"

"That sounds like hell on earth." If nothing else, that whole idea told Ford he was going the right direction. "How's your catering?"

"Exceptional. I'm not doing that right now, though. Right now I'm making pizza."

"I know." Ford rooted through the fridge so he could grab a cream soda. "Is this spoken for?"

"Nope. We're pretty free and easy here. There's enough for everyone."

"Thanks." He pulled up a stool, because Geoff was the first person today to look upon him without the evil fish eye, so Ford thought he would bask in it a bit.

Three huge pizza pans landed on the counter. *Clang. Clang. Clang.* "Did you ever meet Desiree Masters?"

"Uh." Ford blinked a moment, the question such a non sequitur that it threw him. "She was my cousin's bestie, I think."

"Yeah. Good memory. She's my sister."

"No shit?" *Oh, God.* A thousand thoughts tore through him, chief of which was Stoney and Brittany, just as always. Why? How? What the hell? "How's she doing?"

"Good. She's married to a soldier, has seven kids."

"Wow, really? Seven." Damn. Somehow he'd never seen any of Brit's friends settling down and getting off the river.

"I know, right? No river in Fort Hood."

"No kidding." He chuckled, the questions trying to batter their way out. Not about Geoff's sister, but about Stoney. The yeast Geoff mixed with warm water began to work, the smell comforting.

Geoff seemed perfectly at peace in the warm kitchen, like there was a place for a man-bun hippie type in cowboy country. Ford guessed there was if the pizza turned out as good as it began.

Geoff filled all three pans with dough once it rose, and Ford was surprised to find himself still sitting there, drinking coffee and munching a bowl of spiced nuts.

The man was a surprisingly decent conversationalist, knowing a little about damn near everything.

Ford managed not to ask about Stoney for about forty-five minutes. A quick Alfredo went on one pizza, a pesto on one, and red sauce on the third.

Then Geoff grinned at him. "You're killing me. You might as well ask what you really want to."

He went for innocent, because he really wasn't that transparent, was he?

Geoff laughed, the sound bouncing off the cabinets. "Man, lawyers should always look like wolves, not sheep."

"Ah-ooo!" he howled, letting that break the tension a little bit.

A snort of laughter followed, Geoff bleating like a cattleman's wooly nightmare. Lord. He could like this guy.

"He's a good boss, you know, and a great dad. I take it the breakup was bad?"

"You mean me and him?" Ford nodded slowly. "He stayed here, and I left. Then he hooked up with my cousin and had a baby. No recovering from that." The hurt he still felt surprised him. Ford had spent years thinking he was too angry and jaded to be emotional about Stoney, but deep down he was still a confused college kid when it came to Mr. Texas.

"I. Yeah. Yeah, that could be weird." Geoff had the strangest look on his face for a second. "I mean, I can't imagine."

Ford shook it off. "Yeah. It sounds petty, because I love Brit, but I never came back until now."

"No judgment, man. I'm not into that. Things happen for a reason."

"You think so, huh?" He breathed deep when Geoff slid the pizzas into the big double ovens. "If I'm bugging you, holler."

"I love company. I get lonely in here."

"Then I'll hang out a bit." Ford would never have said he was lonesome; he talked to a dozen people a day. He was, though. He knew it now.

People wandered in and out of the kitchen, stealing a cookie here and a cup of coffee there, taking a hug from Geoff and offering him tentative smiles. Ford smiled and nodded and nibbled the antipasto Geoff whipped together.

Quartz came in with a young lady who was only about an inch taller than him.

"Hey, Alanna," Geoff said, and Ford assumed this was the teacher.

"Good afternoon." She gave Geoff a smile, then nudged Quartz's shoulder. "Who is this nice young man, Quartz?"

"Uncle Ford. He's not really my uncle."

"Ford Nixel," Ford said, holding out a hand. "Quartz and I are actually cousins, but I reckon we're of an age for him to call me uncle."

"Mr. Nixel. I'm Alanna Gosfield, the resident tutor."

"Nice to meet you."

"Is there pesto with feta?" Quartz sniffed the air.

"You know it. Alfredo for your dad and Doogie and red sauce for this guy and me."

"I like pesto and feta, very much. Thank you. Can I help make salads?"

"You may." Geoff set Quartz to chopping with a weird glass vegetable knife, leaving Ford with Alanna.

"It's nice to meet you. You're Mr. Ty's nephew?"

"I am. He called me and asked me to come have a look around." Ford kept his tone light and watched Quartz with half his attention.

"That's lovely. I'm sure you'll have fun while you're here."

Quartz focused on the task at hand, totally uninterested in his surroundings, in the company. The little boy didn't look a thing like Stoney, or Brittany either, to be honest.

"I'm sure I will. Used to love it here." He stifled his sigh. He could love it again, damn it.

"Well, it's a beautiful place." Alanna patted his arm. "Do you have children?"

"No." He gave her a sideways glance. "You?"

"Not yet."

What the heck did that mean? He checked out her ring finger, then realized he could be giving the wrong impression. Really, he was just nosy.

He was the queerest man in Western Colorado, for fuck's sake.

She chuckled. "No, I am not married, but I do have a long-term guy."

"Nice." Geoff winked at them. "I am single, though."

"Are you?" Ford asked.

"And he's gay. He only dates boys," Quartz pronounced.

"Yep. I like 'em big and hairy." Geoff twirled.

Was this really happening?

"Why?" Quartz asked.

"Because everyone has a type. You'll grow up to find yours."

"Is it okay if I like girls?" Quartz glanced at Ford, looking uneasy. "Dad likes boys, and Angie likes girls, but I think I like girls."

"That is perfectly okay," Ford said. "You love who you love."

Wait. Dad likes boys? What the ever-loving fuck?

"He's right," Alanna said. "In this day and age there's no way anyone can tell you who to care for. You can like boys and girls, if you want."

"Yeah." Geoff gave them all an arch look. "Just remember there are some folks who don't believe that, and sometimes you have to be careful."

"Some people are bigots." Quartz wrinkled his nose.

"Yep. They're taught that way from birth." Ford liked these people, damn it.

"That's stupid, huh, Geoff?"

"Yessir."

Lord, this kid needed some social skills. Still, while he didn't look like Brittany at all, he reminded Ford a lot of her.

"Where's Daddy?"

"He's probably working, Quartz," Alanna said.

"Can I go tell him lunch is almost ready?"

"Wash your hands," Geoff said. "What kind of dressing?"

"Ranch. Everyone is obsessed with my hands."

"Kids have gross hands," Stoney said, walking right in and heading to the sink without a glance at Ford. "Smells amazing."

"Pizza."

"I do not have gross hands, Daddy!"

"Yep. Covered in funk and foul. I'm surprised anyone grows to adulthood." The tease was easy, gentle, and Quartz laughed happily and then hugged Stoney tight. As soon as Quartz touched him, Stoney squealed. "Eew! Boy germs!"

Ford chuckled, drawing a surprised glance from Stoney.

He shrugged. It was cute, and Stoney was a great dad, obviously.

And into boys, his son said. The ridiculous flare of hope that gave Ford made him feel like the biggest fool on earth. No fool like an old one, right?

Stoney went to sit at the farthest edge of the table from him, next to Alanna, nodding to her, to the rough-looking cowboy sitting with her.

Yeah. Idiot. Ford would have just left, but Geoff was making this pizza because of him.

The wrangler, Angie, wandered in with another woman who wore flannel and jeans and boots. "Thanks for texting, Geoff. Smells so much better than Totino's."

"Anytime."

"Hetty!" Stoney stood up, and the little butch woman headed right over and gave Stoney a hug.

"How's that new yearling settling in? You being good to her?"

"Shit, yes. We'll go look after lunch."

"Good deal. Who's this?" Hetty asked.

Ford stood to shake hands. "Ford Nixel."

"Ah. You're the lawyer. I've heard tell of you." She shook, and it was like shaking hands with a trucker. Christ.

Ford grinned, trying not to roll his eyes. "I did grow up on the ranch, though. I hear you breed horses."

"I do. Mostly Belgians, but I supply these hooligans with what they need."

"We need to chat." Ford ignored Stoney's grim expression.

"Sure. Holler when you and the boss got a minute."

Ford looked at Stoney, who nodded reluctantly. *Progress. Woo-hoo.*

He didn't miss for a second that Hetty made her position on who the boss was crystal clear either. Ford did wonder if she'd been that way with Ty too. He'd have to ask.

Geoff pulled pizzas out of the oven, then began cutting the thick, crunchy crust. Ford's mouth watered. *Oh, God, look at that.* The smell of cheese and basil and peppery meat was fucking perfect.

Geoff dished up, the perfect two pieces per person, one for the kiddo, with salad. Damn. The crust had this buttery thing going on…. *Yum.*

He thought about just dying of pure bliss. Also, he considered stealing Geoff away as his own private chef.

Nah. He'd need the man for the kinds of guests he wanted to bring in. He'd just have to eat at the ranch often.

Still, it was good to know Geoff could please the most discerning palate. The crunch when he bit into the pizza made him grunt happily, the cheese stringing off when he pulled the slice away from his mouth. The first few minutes had nothing but munching and crunching, then the soft buzz of chatter—mostly Quartz's—began.

Ford felt a momentary pang of guilt for intruding on this group, so obviously a family, so clearly not his. He stood abruptly, mumbling an apology, and left the room, needing to be somewhere else.

Geoff was almost immediately right there. "Was the pizza not right, honey? I can try again."

Ford looked down at his hands, which were pizza-less. "I was just going to take it to eat in the office. I forgot it, huh? It's amazing." God, he was turning into a blithering idiot. He did that, according to all of his exes. Well, all the ones he talked to. He freaked out and ran.

"Uh-huh. You know, it's cool. You don't know anyone anymore. It's okay to feel wigged."

"I used to live here. What happened? I don't even know anymore." Ford laughed harshly. "The pizza is epic, though."

"Shit, man. Life happens to the best of us." To his utter shock, Geoff grabbed him and hugged him, held him tight, like they were friends.

He hugged back, just starved enough for a little comfort to go for it.

Geoff held on, letting him breathe and calm himself down before letting go. "I'll bring you your pizza, dude."

"Thank you. I appreciate it." And that was no bullshit.

"No worries." Geoff sent him off and arrived a few minutes later with his pizza, salad, and a plate of peanut butter cookies.

"You rock, man."

Geoff nodded. "I do. Totally. Holler if you need anything. Text me." Geoff scribbled a number on the blotter on Ty's desk.

"Thanks. I will." He might just surprise himself by texting Geoff sometime soon.

"Good deal." Geoff grinned at him, eyes warm and friendly and genuine as hell. "Supper is at six thirty. I'm making lasagna, and there's ice cream sundaes for dessert."

"I'll be there unless you think it will drive everyone away." He chuckled. "If you think I will, I'll take it in here."

"You'll be fine, man. You can't be part of the family if the family doesn't know you."

"Right." Yeah, because everyone wanted him to fit right in. Ford winked, knowing it had to be a little lame.

"Trust me, man. It's going to get better."

"Thanks." He needed to get back to work and quit feeling sorry for himself.

Being here was…. Maybe it was more than he could cope with. He closed his eyes and took a deep breath, the air in the office scented with garlic and cheese now.

The pizza really was epic.

Stoney wandered through the hallway about twenty minutes later, mail in hand. "Ty wanting me to leave the business mail for you?"

"I'd like to go over anything with you that I need to learn." There. That was neutral, right? "And I definitely need to see any taxes and such."

Stoney shrugged. "I'm not sure I got anything I can teach you, so far as the business goes, but holler if you got questions, and I'll find you someone who can answer."

"You know the ranch better than me." He studied Stoney carefully, trying to see the college boy he'd known in the man.

"You'll remember. It hasn't changed much." Stoney looked tired, unhappy, and Ford had to wonder whether the lines around the man's mouth had appeared when he had.

"The house looks good." Inane, but true. The new wing was amazing from the outside, at least.

"It does. Quartz loves it. He doesn't remember being anywhere else."

"Was he somewhere else?" Ford had to admit he was damned curious.

"Sure. He lived with his mom until she died. She had a condo in Carbondale. Closer to the tourists."

"Oh." Ford frowned. "You didn't live with her?"

"Nope. I lived in the bunkhouse like everyone else."

"Why?" It popped out, and Ford waved a hand. "Sorry. None of mine."

Stoney gave him a weird look, totally confused. "It ain't a secret."

"I thought you two were a thing." Now Ford was really frowning.

Stoney rolled his eyes. "Yeah, because I'm going to... whatever. Holler if you need me. I got to exercise horses if we ain't gonna have folks to do it."

"Hey, what am I supposed to think? You tell me to shove off, and then you're having a kid with my cousin?"

"I guess you think just what you think, man. That's fine with me."

"God, you're still fucking infuriating." Ford shook his head, his anger still right below the surface when it came to Stoney, shocking him.

"I'm no different than I ever was, Ford. I'm just a cowboy."

"You—" He closed his eyes, taking a deep breath. "Yeah. Is it going to be a problem if I come to dinner? I don't want to upset the routine."

"Ford, it's your fucking ranch. You got controlling interest. If you don't want me there, I'll beg off for a day or two, but you ain't going nowhere, and I have a little boy to raise. Get over it."

Ford stared at Stoney, absolutely certain he'd never even known this man. "I wasn't asking you to beg off. I just want to be able to eat supper without feeling as if I've driven everyone away." He was fucking trying to be nice.

"Fair enough." Stoney watched him like a hawk.

"Yeah." His head was starting to pound. "I miss her, you know. Brit."

"She was a damn good friend, but the river owned her, body and soul."

"It did." That they could agree on. Brittany had loved the river beyond all things. Ford burned with questions he didn't ask. A friend. Did friends have kids together?

"I got to hustle. No rest for the wicked."

"Sure. See you at supper." He needed to start out like he could hold out, and he and Stoney had to put on a single front for the guests once they began arriving.

"Uh-huh."

Laconic asshole.

Ford watched Stoney leave, then shook his head. This situation was going to test his last nerve.

Good thing he was... shit, he didn't know. The nerviest guy he knew? The man with the most nerves. Whatever.

He just needed to get his shit together and figure out what to do.

That was easier said than done, especially when he felt totally out of place. He'd figure it out. That was his other magic power. Ford got shit done.

Chapter Eight

STONEY ended up begging off supper in favor of being one with the bottle, and breakfast in favor of worshipping at the porcelain throne.

Okay, so that didn't help a goddamn thing. It just left him scoured out and headachy. Still, he'd given Ford a couple meals on his own, and he could just grab coffee and get to work. Geoff should be out milking goats or something by now, and Stoney could crawl into the kitchen and get a coffee and a piece of toast.

Christ have mercy, his brain was going to explode.

The coast was clear in the kitchen, so he ducked in. Stoney popped bread into the toaster and pulled out a pod to make coffee in the fancy little brew machine Geoff loved.

He flipped through his e-mails on his phone, then his texts, pleased when there wasn't a whole lot of nothing. He might survive today after all.

Then Ford walked into the damned kitchen, handsome face like a thundercloud, and Stoney knew his parade was about to get rained on like whoa.

Good thing he was waterproof as all fuck.

"So, guess you skipped dinner and breakfast just to make me feel better?" Ford scowled harder, and if he wasn't wearing a pair of sweats and a T-shirt with a *Dr. Who* logo, he might be scary.

"I drank my supper and puked through breakfast, but thanks for asking." *Fuck-head.*

"Why the hell did you do that? Don't you have a kid?"

"Last time I checked." Like he was drunk around Quartz. Fuck that shit. Quartz was spending the night with his best friend, Bennie, in Glenwood. They had plans to go to the hot springs and hike up to Doc Holliday's grave.

"Well, what am I supposed to think?" Ford was ramping up. Oh, the guy was all class; he'd never been a shouter. But Ford was getting all Western on him, assuming a credible cowboy stance. Someone must have given him lessons, because he sure as fuck hadn't stood like a bull rider back in the day.

"It ain't none of yours, one way or the t'other."

"Bullshit." The word cracked out like a walnut being stepped on by a dinosaur.

He didn't respond; he simply let one eyebrow lift as he stared. Stoney had stared down way scarier things than Ford Nixel.

"I need you to be in on this, Stoney." Ford wasn't pleading, Stoney could tell. He was stating fact. "You and Ty will lose the ranch otherwise."

"Have I slacked in my job today? In any way?" He kept his voice even. It was easier to get close enough to clock a man that way.

"Not the wrangler part. Too bad your head is too far up your ass to see you need to act like an owner," Ford sneered.

"You mean the part where you sit in the office or the part where you pretend that you remember anything about this ranch?"

"Fuck you! I fucking grew up here. I love this place. I always have." Ford shocked the shit out of him by shouting.

"Then you might ought to show up every now and again."

"You made it pretty clear you didn't want to see me, and Ty made it perfectly clear he'd rather have a stranger around than me." Ford shut down; Stoney saw it happen, just like it always had. His expression cooled, became guarded, which meant he was about to turn tail and run.

It was a shame; playing with pissed Ford would be more fun. He wasn't smart enough to spar with Mr. Top of His Class in Law School.

"Enough of the ancient history. God knows I don't want to know how you hooked up with Brit. Ty wanted me to try to help keep the ranch for you and Quartz, and I will, but I can't do it if you fight me."

"I've spoken to you twice." He was fairly sure that didn't count as fighting.

Ford stared at him for a moment, a muscle jumping in his jaw. "Fuck. Right. Have a good hangover."

"Look, what the fuck do you want? What are you up to?" Stoney wasn't even 100 percent sure why he asked, but he did it anyway. He couldn't buy Ford out, he couldn't imagine moving Quartz, so he had to figure… something.

"Ty called me. This place is important. It needs improvements, needs a new plan. I'm not up to anything."

"So what do you want?" It was a fair question.

"I don't know." Ford laughed, the sound strained but seemingly genuine.

"Oh." He guessed that was fair. "You want coffee?"

"Please. I have to drive into Aspen in a bit and deal with some tax shit for a client."

That sounded like pure hell.

He grabbed the pod dealie and popped it in, fixing Ford a cup. He automatically added cream to it, then half a teaspoon of sugar. When Stoney handed over the cup, Ford was staring at him, eyes wide.

"You remember."

"Sure I do." He remembered every single thing about Ford. The bastard had been his Mr. Right, and it had torn out most of his heart when Ford had gone back to school without even trying to talk to him. Just packed up in the middle of the night and left.

"You—" Ford cut himself off. "I'm sorry, man, I just don't get it."

"Get it?" What was there to get?

"Why—I mean, what happened? Why the hell did you break up with me and stay here and…. What the hell was with you and Brit?"

"I was failing out of school. They were about to make me leave. Ty offered me a job." And there was no way to fix the fact that he was too fucking slow to make it in Ford's world.

"What?" Ford actually stepped toward him, scowling. "Why wouldn't you tell me?"

"Tell you what? That I was a fuckup? You figured that out."

"No, what I figured out was that you wanted a ranch more than you wanted me." Ford's mouth twisted.

"I needed a job. I got one."

"You sure did." Ford took the coffee in hand. "There's leftovers in the fridge. Pancakes and bacon. Talk atcha later."

He didn't bother answering. What the hell was he supposed to do? He hated this shit, but he was who he was.

The dumb cowboy.

At least he had a boy who was the neatest kid in the world, the best thing that had ever happened to him. He wouldn't jeopardize that for anything. So, no more getting his drunk on—at least not where the asshole owner could catch him.

Stoney grinned, feeling good enough to heat up some of Geoff's amazing pancakes for a post-toast snack.

His phone rang on the way to the fridge, and he grabbed it. "Boss? Boss, we got a hunting group coming in tomorrow. I need you in the office."

"Be there in two shakes of a dead lamb's tail." Lord have mercy, time to get to work. Stoney grabbed his toast, his coffee, and his phone and headed out to the office. He had to decide what to do with those hunters.

Ford could wait.

Chapter Nine

FORD needed a big bottle of water. His head was gonna explode, and he had a meeting with a client regarding tax law in about ten minutes.

He was still fifteen minutes from his office.

Ford keyed his hands-free. "Call the Aspen office."

The phone rang, and Eileen answered. "You're late. Don't kill yourself. Mr. Porter's running an hour late, and your 11:00 a.m. canceled."

"Oh, thank you." He chuckled. "I had a rough night. Didn't sleep."

"What can I do? Mr. Porter's already on the road."

"No, no, I'm ten minutes away. I'll be there in two shakes." What did that even mean? He'd picked up the expression at school, he thought. From Stoney.

God damn it.

He had managed not to have that motherfucker on his mind for years, just the occasional pang when Ty said something in an e-mail about the ranch. Now he was caught in a loop that revolved around the stupid son of a bitch. Who clearly still thought about him not at all. Not if he was getting drunk instead of coming to supper.

Or breakfast.

Jesus.

Just what the ranch needed—a co-owner with a drinking problem. Ford rolled his eyes. Ty assured him Stoney wasn't a drunk, but Stoney wasn't proving anything good.

Hell, so far the one good thing was the man seemed to be a reasonably competent father. Quartz wasn't the most socially apt kid, but he was polite and clearly pretty smart, and the staff adored him.

Maybe he should grab a coffee and a pastry before he went in. Eileen would love that.

He had an hour, right? There was an organic coffee place two blocks from his office…. Man, he'd been sad to see that little goddess restaurant in Carbondale had closed. No more cheesy melty things…. Rats.

Ford parked and headed in, tugging his jacket closed against the wind. Man, it was cooling down fast this year.

"Ford? Hey, buddy, what the hell are you doing up here?" Matt Gregson strode up to him, hand out to shake. Square, callused, that hand took him back to high school in a heartbeat.

Ford grinned. "Lord. Matt. I should ask you that. I thought Aspen was too froufrou for you."

"Oh, shit. You know me. I follow the money. I'm doing entertainment law. You'd be surprised how well that works here."

"Nah. Lots of actors and all." Ford never kept track of who was in Aspen anymore. He did just fine for himself without all the drama. "Gonna get a coffee if you want to come with."

"I was heading that way. You still in Santa Fe mostly?" Matt was the personification of the middle-aged former football star, muscle heading gently to fat, mostly good-natured, but with enough competitive edge left that he could enjoy law.

"Yeah. Uncle Ty, he had to move to the Junction, so I'm up to help with the ranch."

"Rock on! You'll have to meet me for supper one night. There's a little bunch of us that get together once a month or so."

"No shit?" Ford chuckled at the idea. He'd never been one to revisit the past, but why not? "Sounds good."

"I'll e-mail you the deets. It's informal. Just me, Kenny Barter, Buck and Vic Harrison, and then Mike Beals."

"The twins are still in town?" Both of them? Those boys had been beautiful, and the fantasy subject of some very inappropriate teenaged jack-off sessions.

Matt snorted. "Shit, they'll never leave the Roaring Fork. They'd die under five thousand feet."

"True. They still climbing fourteeners?"

"You know it. That's their whole lives." They moved forward with the line, getting closer to the pastry case. "They never married, had kids, anything. They climb."

"I know they had some sponsor just out of high school." North Face, maybe. Something like that. Ford admired the stick-with-it-ness of the guys, for sure.

"Yeah. I don't get it, but they haven't changed a bit."

"Some of us can't say that, huh?" Ford elbowed Matt in the ribs, the teenager back in force.

"Lord, no." Matt patted his belly. "Sharon says that she's the one that's pregnant, but I'm carrying the weight for this one."

"How many does that make?" Ford vaguely remembered Matt had two kids the last time they'd seen each other.

"This is number four, and I think we've decided to stop there."

"Wow. Four." Sometimes Ford felt a real pang of sorrow over the idea that he'd never have kids. Which, okay, weird, because he was queer and a bit of a loner and probably utterly not dad material, but whatever. It was what it was.

"So, what'll you two have today?" asked the barista, and Ford ordered a double shot mocha with caramel drizzle and extra whip for Eileen and an almond milk latte for him, along with two huge apple turnovers.

"I'm going for the white chocolate mocha and a lemon poppy seed slice, please."

"You got it. Together?" She looked them over with a jaded glance.

"I'm buying, yes," Ford said without batting an eye.

"Thanks, man. I'll pick up the next one." The best thing about Matt was that it was the truth. The man had the memory of an elephant.

"Deal," Ford agreed. He was really enjoying Matt's company. The day was improving.

They lined up against the wall, waiting for their drinks. He needed to remember this. He didn't belong on the ranch anymore. He belonged out here where there were lattes and people who didn't act like he was the big bad wolf.

Lord have mercy.

He was losing his mind.

"So, anyway, text me your number, and I'll holler when we're gonna get together next," Matt said before handing him a business card.

"Will do. It'll be good to see everyone, catch up." Had he gotten to that age? The catching-up age? He skipped reunions and weddings…. Maybe he was. Or at least at the right place in his life.

"It will." Matt grabbed his drink and pastry when it came up. "Okay, I have to get on. Good to see you, man."

"Have a good day." He headed back to the car, feeling lighter, like maybe it wasn't him. Maybe Stoney just sucked.

He could handle that. Blame Stoney. Wasn't that a song?

If it wasn't, it sure as shit would be now.

Chapter Ten

"**DADDY!**" Quartz's voice rang out as Stoney stomped the mud off his boots. He'd been out with that early hunting party for the last three days, and he was filthy, exhausted, and cold down to the bone. When had early October gotten so cold?

Still, he could no more resist that happy cry now than he ever could. "Hey, buddy boy. How goes it?"

"Good! I made my roller coaster! Wanna see?"

"Of course I do. Let me get my jacket off. Did it snow here at the house? It sprinkled on me up on the mountain."

"No." Quartz wrinkled his nose. "It just rained, and I couldn't ride."

"That's no fun, man. Tell me about your roller coaster." He could listen and get clean at the same time.

"It has three loop-de-loops!" Quartz chattered at him, bouncing.

"Three? Man, that's intense." He turned on the shower and got the steam billowing out.

"It is! Then you go up a hill and twist coming down like a helix thingee."

"What did you fabricate it out of?" Oh. Hot water. Thank God. Soap.

"I used some of your old Erector Set and some pieces of scrap stuff Geoff gave me from the garden fencing and—he's making meatloaf tonight. Can you stop him?"

"I can't, but I bet that Geoff remembers that meatloaf is your least favorite ever and has an alternative." He'd bet Geoff would, in fact, never forget the reaction six-year old Quartz had.

"Oh. Okay." Quartz brightened. "Maybe a sloppy joe!"

"Maybe. Maybe a peanut butter sandwich, though, because he cooked already, right?"

Quartz handled disappointment less than well.

"Okay. Maybe with his strawberry jam."

"He always has that." Geoff canned. A lot. Like, as in him and Ty had built on a pantry room. A room.

The jam and jelly room with a shelf for pickles and one for tomatoes. There were two upright freezers for corn and green chiles and more.

"We eat pretty good, huh?" Stoney said, ruffling Quartz's hair.

"Yeah. Except for meatloaf."

"Right. Except for meatloaf." The kid was obsessed. Stoney got it. He loathed liver and onions. Too bad Geoff was obsessed with finding a meatloaf Quartz would eat.

A guy had to live with a kid 24-7 before he understood that some battles weren't worth fighting. "Hand me my shirt, bud."

"Yes, sir. I'm glad you're home, Daddy."

"Lord, son. Me too. My ass is getting too old for this shit."

"Is the rest of you old too?"

"Some parts are more used up than others, that's for sure." No shit on that. He hadn't gotten laid in eight years. Those parts were still under fucking warranty.

"I think you're cool, Daddy."

Oh. Well, that was good to hear. "Thank you. I think you're pretty damn spiffy yourself. Come on. I need to see this roller coaster."

"Yes!" Quartz led him to their sitting room. "Ta-da!"

The thing was stunning—a Frankensteiny mishmash of a zillion scrapped parts, half a dozen motorized gizmos and a metric fuckton of old Christmas lights that took up the front room floor.

Stoney was in love. He clapped. "Oh, man. Look at this!"

Quartz beamed, then glanced at the clock. "I can show you how it works after supper. I bet you're hungry."

"Uh-huh. Still. Just once, huh? One quick run?"

"Woo!" Quartz grabbed a train set remote and flicked a switch. The tiny train cars started up the hill, climbing with rattles and shudders, but climbing nonetheless.

Stoney made all kinds of mental notes for later, but he always kept his mouth shut on the first run.

The first runs of one of his brilliant boy's inventions were to enjoy and just go with the shock and awe. The practical parts would come later.

Stoney cheered when the car made all the loops and ended on the helix. "High five!"

Quartz squealed and slapped his hand, pride just glowing from his boy. "It worked!"

"Totally. It totally works. You rock, son. Swear to God."

"Thanks, Daddy!" Quartz hugged him, the move spontaneous enough to make Stoney's eyes burn. "Do you think Geoff made pie?"

"Maybe meatloaf pie!"

Quartz made gagging noises, but that was it. No fits, no panic—just kid reactions. Excellent. Maybe it was like the doctors had said and it would start to get easier now that he was getting older. Stoney had never worked so hard at not losing his temper as he had when he became a daddy. Most of the time he managed. Most of the time.

He stood, stretching. Okay, supper. Then collapsing on the couch with a nice *NCIS* marathon.

They headed to the main kitchen, the smell of meatloaf filling the air and making Stoney's belly rumble. He'd never tell Quartz, but Geoff's meatloaf made him super happy.

"Boss!" Geoff winked. "Didn't expect you back. Looks like you'll have to eat Quartz's meatloaf and he can have something else."

"I am so totally in." He moved in to give Geoff a man hug, but Geoff wouldn't have it, hugging him like they were best friends who hadn't seen each other in a coon's age.

Quartz poked him.

"Ow. So, what does Quartz eat, then, buddy?"

"I made him sloppy joes. Is that cool?"

Quartz's crow proved that someone was off the kid's shit list.

"I think he approves." Stoney chuckled. "What can we do?"

"Quartz, can you pull out the salad dressings? You get you a cup of coffee, boss. You look like you could use it."

"Thanks." He desperately needed a boost if he was going to make it through supper. The hunting party hadn't been bad, but the heavy clouds and the mud and the constant snoring from three guys who hadn't bathed in days wore at him.

"Hey, guys." Angie wandered in, her hat in hand. "Man, it's wet."

"Gonna snow tonight, I can feel it in my bones."

"Yeah?" She snorted. "Your old-old bones."

"Hush, you old broad. Who else is coming for supper?"

"My wife. Leon. Abner."

"The farrier?" Stoney chuckled. The meatloaf brought folks out of the woodwork.

"There's German chocolate cake for dessert, man."

"Oh God. No wonder everyone is coming." Geoff's cake kept him going in the darkest of times.

"The more the merrier." Geoff grinned. The man just loved to feed people, even if he wouldn't eat his own meatloaf.

Could you make a tofu loaf?

Oh, God. That sounded like ketchup-covered hell. He tried not to gag, because Geoff would get all offended.

Angie got out the cutlery, he grabbed plates, and Geoff started bringing food to the big old table.

The kitchen door banged open just about the time he was about to say grace, Ford blowing in like a stiff arctic wind. "God, it smells good in here."

"It's time for grace, Uncle Ford. Sit down." Ah, his direct boy.

"Gotcha." Ford seemed like he was in a fine mood, grinning at one and all, even Stoney.

"Dear Lord, bless the food, the ranch, and all the cowboys, big and small." He glanced at Quartz, who always had a special request.

"And all the horses, especially Mousey who has a hurt hoof."

"And all the horses, especially Mousey. In Jesus' name we pray."

They all nodded. "Amen."

They dug in, everyone humming at the mushroom gravy flavor of the meatloaf. No sad ketchup shit here. The sloppy joes were a hit with Quartz, and no one pointed out that Geoff was eating them too, so they must be vegan crumbles. Sloppy falafels?

Whatever. He wasn't going to be all "you must eat all the meat" and shit on his boy, because, well, he guessed because that was his dad in a nutshell, and also he didn't run cattle, so it wasn't like that was the food in abundance.

That would be venison and elk, both of which Quartz ate fairly easily.

"You look as tickled as a man with a feather up his butt," Geoff told Ford.

"I am. I renewed the BLM lease today."

Everyone went quiet for a long second, then the cheering started, the congratulations. Man, this crew could make some noise.

"Oh man, you're our hero!" Angie gushed, slapping Ford on the back, and Stoney bit back the urge to snarl.

Fact was, he hadn't managed it. If he had, Ty wouldn't have brought Ford in, so it was only fair to give the man his due.

Would have been nice to know before the rest of the staff, maybe, but whatever.

Ford glanced at him, smile fading a bit. "Thanks. That last meeting today did it, but they grilled me like a sirloin."

"Well, that's why Ty brought you in, right? You're the man for the job." Geoff beamed. "You get to pick supper tomorrow night, man, for saving all our bacon."

"Daddy?" Quartz looked up at him. "Is everything okay?"

"Huh? Sure it is. That's just what we wanted to happen. Now we can get back to working."

"Oh, good." Quartz nodded, and Stoney forced a wide grin. His kid was so frickin' good at gauging his mood.

"If you have time tomorrow, Stoney, we can meet, and I can fill you in."

"Sure, man. Just tell me when you want me. I'll be around." There was no way on earth he was going to be within earshot of Ford Nixel tomorrow. No fucking way. He was going to go find something impossible and physical that would keep him busy and out of trouble.

Right now he was so mad—mostly at himself, if he was going to be honest, and he tended toward that— that he could smack Ford right in the face.

Ford stared him down, as if the man knew exactly what he was thinking. "We'll make it seven so I can catch you before you head out."

Fucker.

"Sure, boss. No sweat." Maybe Ford could give him a list of duties too. Muck out the stables. Haul the dirties to the laundry room. Oh, maybe even worm the horses. That would be a good job for him. Something nice and easy.

Geoff and Angie watched them like a tennis match, and the others tucked in to their food, heads down.

Ford just shook his head, grabbing his plate. "Well, I just wanted to tell everyone. I've got a bunch of reports to finish up in the office. Thanks for supper, Geoff."

"Oh, for fuck's sake, man. This is your motherfucking ranch; quit acting like it's not and sit down and eat your goddamn food with the staff like a decent human being."

"Daddy!"

He shot Quartz a look, and to his son's credit, he knew to shut up and eat his supper.

"Half mine," Ford said, putting on what Stoney always thought of as his lawyer face. He'd had it in college too. "I'm well aware that you wish it were otherwise, but I'm doing the best I can, given the circumstances."

He didn't respond with anything more than a stare. He knew that nothing pissed Ford off more than silence. The man could argue his way out of anything, but if Stoney didn't give him ammunition, Ford was firing blanks.

That meant the bastard had to be a lot closer to do damage.

"Guys. Guys, wow. Intense. That's rough on digestion." Geoff, the eternal peacekeeper, offered Ford a grin. "Come sit. I have the world's best cake dialed up."

Ford sat, nibbling at his supper, head held high. Stoney wasn't backing down, though. This was his place too, and Quartz needed to see he was willing to work for it.

God, he was so fucking wore that he didn't have his own head on straight. The nights of sitting up against a pine tree with a knife and a piece of wood that was either going to be a Christmas tree or a rocket ship were catching up with him.

Geoff patted his leg under the table, and he had to smile. Their Geoff did hate strife.

Quartz ate quickly, shoveling the food in. "Can I have cake soon, Daddy? The roller coaster is waiting."

"When Geoff serves it, yep." He managed to eat about a quarter of his meatloaf, but that was it. He'd warm it up for breakfast. Maybe even a late-night snack.

"Cake it is." Geoff took a huge load of dishes away with him, then came back with a cake stand. "Quartz, buddy, can you get the dessert plates?"

"Yes, sir." Quartz hopped up and Stoney tried to see if he could find his future in the dregs of a cup of coffee.

Angie kicked him. Hard. When his head snapped up, she winked at him. Evil woman.

He made sure Quartz couldn't see him, and then he flipped her off, making the motion slow and deliberate.

She hooted with laughter, drawing a stare from Ford. Who she stuck her tongue out at. "Christ. You boys are thick."

"I will take you to the woodshed, woman," Stoney said.

"I'd be the one that left, though, Skeletor." Angie didn't even pretend to look sad.

Ford surprised him by chuckling, the sound rusty as all get-out. "No one told me ranch life was like high school as an adult."

"Shit, man. Everything is like high school. Didn't they teach you that in law school?" Hetty's voice was dry as dust and twice as raspy.

"Nope. Unless I fell asleep between torts and contract law and it was there."

"What the ever loving fuck is a tort? Isn't that a cake?" Angie was totally willing to be the voice of redneckedness.

"No, dork. It's a civil legal wrongdoing that doesn't cover contracts." When everyone stared, Geoff shrugged. "What? I read things."

"Liar. You saw it on *Law and Order*." God knew he and Geoff had had more than their fair share of Netflix-a-thons.

"TV, reading, six of one," Geoff said, grinning over at him.

Ford rolled his eyes. "So useful, those law shows."

Stoney could get that. Some of the "cowboy" shit he saw made him want to spit nails. Angie read these crazy cowboy books by some chick from New York City. Aloud. At staff meetings.

Like any cowboy worth his salt had time to wax poetic about shit. Fuck that. Romance was cleaning the manure off your boots before you came inside, paying the electric bill on time, and making sure your kid brushed his goddamn teeth.

Ford was laughing at something Doc said, and Stoney took the chance to look a little. He didn't think Ford cracked up like that much. Of course, Doc had been here way longer than he had. Possibly longer than the mountains had been.

Shame. It was a good look on the man.

Ford caught his eye, the smile staying in place this time, and Stoney found himself grinning a bit in return. *Huh*.

That was probably a bad fucking idea. The last thing Stoney needed was Ford knowing there was a torch that might still burn some. It did, late at night when it was just him and his hand, but Ford could butt right out on that.

The cake went down easier than supper, though, didn't it? Geoff was a king among men.

He grabbed another huge cup of coffee and his leftovers for the morning. The conversation sounded like road noise. "You ready, son?"

"Yessir." Quartz hopped up and took his plate to the sink.

"Y'all have a good one."

"Night." The chorus of good nights sounded, echoed by Ford, who watched him closely.

"Night. Come on, Quartz."

The hallway seemed longer than ever.

Chapter Eleven

FORD woke up the next morning and reached for his bedside lamp. Which wasn't there. This old brass bed had a reading lamp clipped on the top.

Man, he needed to move in some of his shit.

The thought shocked him, but not as much as it would have just last night. Much as he hated to admit it, Stoney was right. This was his place, and he belonged here. Why was he commuting in from Aspen and staying in a guest room?

Half of this house was his, dammit. Half of the ranch. And God knew he'd just pitched a whole new ball of wax to the BLM folks, one he hadn't even told Stoney about. That was Stoney's own fault too, not wanting to act like a ranch owner. Ty had been counting on the lazy son of a bitch. Okay, not lazy, but shiftless. Shiftless for sure and possibly drunk.

He'd seen Stoney's eyes last night, all bloodshot and barely open. And the man was raising his nephew. His sort of nephew. His cousin's little boy. Whatever.

Ford heard a scraping in the hallway, something banging against the bedroom door, and he rose and padded over to peer out.

There were a pair of good old boys hauling out a dresser, and he heard his uncle's voice. "Take these boxes too, guys, but leave the bed."

Ford grabbed his robe and headed out. "Ty?"

"Hey, son. How goes it?" Ty looked happy, healthy, almost perky.

"Fine. What's up?" Had Ty even been planning to let him know he was there for the rest of his stuff?

"I found these fine men last night, and they had an opening today, so instead of waiting for another three weeks, I struck while the iron was hot, so to speak."

"Ah." Well, that was better, right? Spontaneous, not evil.

"Besides, this is easier. Rip the bandage off, yeah?"

"I guess. You want me to keep your room set up for when you visit?"

"Nope. If I stay, I can use Stoney's guest room. That way you can make it yours."

"Jesus. You don't even want to stay on my side of the hall? Do I have leprosy?" That wasn't fair, but damn. He could fix up a fucking guest room for Ty.

Ty fastened a look on him that could have frozen hell. "Pardon me? What exactly is that supposed to mean?"

"It means I can't get Stoney to even look at me for five minutes when you fucking asked me to come here and help. I need his ass on board, and he's playing drunk cowboy asshole!" Ford was sick and tired of playing nice.

"You hold it right there." Ty grabbed his phone and dialed. "Boy, you get over to my office. Right now. No. Now."

Then the phone clicked shut and Ty pointed. "In my office."

Fucking great. Just what he needed. A stern talking to was going to make things *so* much better.

Ty whacked him with the phone.

"Ow!"

"What did I say? Office. Now."

"I'm not even dressed." Ford went, though, didn't he? Wasn't an old guy on dialysis supposed to be weak?

Stoney came running in, covered in mud and snow and horseshit. "What's wrong? Did something bad happen?"

"What the fuck are you two doing?" Ty demanded. "Why are your heads up your asses?"

Stoney blinked at Ty, then at him. "What?"

"You heard me! This ranch will go down if you two don't get your shit together."

"Hey! I got the BLM renewal." Ford was doing his part.

"Which is what I brought you in here for, not to fight with Stoney."

"I ain't fought with no one." Stoney's voice was flat, dangerously still.

"Don't go there. What the fuck are you about, boy? Drinking on the job? What are you thinking? You know better!"

"What? When? When have I done that?" Now he had Stoney's full attention. Like 100 percent.

"Ford says you were drunk."

Ford rolled his eyes. "He was. And he's been hungover at work more than once. You forget that my main complaint is that he refuses to work and or meet with me, and time is wasting."

"No, sir." Stoney stood up tall—as tall as he could—and shook his head. "I had a couple of drinks one evening when Quartz was spending the night away, and I paid for it that next morning and missed breakfast, but that was it. Absolutely it. Last time I checked, I was legal and weren't nobody hurt by me having a few."

"What about dinner last night?" Ford demanded. "You were bloodshot as hell."

"I hadn't slept in three days. I was working a hunting party." Stoney looked at him like he was a bug smashed on the bottom of his boot before turning to his uncle. "What else, Ty? Let's just get it over with. I got work to do."

"Why didn't Ford know you were out with a hunting party? You need to be having weekly meetings, at least." Ty was getting too red in the face, too out of breath. Damn it.

"Yes, sir. I'll have Ford get me a schedule when he'll be available." That wall was huge, just this blank, emotionless thing.

God, he hated that. Hated it. His hands clenched. "Ty, go on and get your stuff moved. I'm moving in permanently tomorrow, so I can chase Stoney around on horseback if I have to."

"You two boys have to work together!" Ty blustered, and it was Stoney who eased him down into a chair, got him a glass of water. "I'm serious. You can't be at odds; you'll ruin this place. You're family, for God's sake."

Family. Shit. That was the one thing they'd never managed to be. Fuck buddies? Sure. Ex-fuck buddies definitely. He got the feeling Stoney hated him. Ford wished he could return the favor.

"Family, are we? Excellent." Stoney spun from where he was and clocked him, fist crashing into his jaw like a sledgehammer, sending him flat out on the floor, his bell rung. "You ever tell another lie about me, *brother*, and I swear by all I hold holy no one will ever find the body. I ain't a drunk, I ain't a slouch, and I ain't your motherfucking employee. I'm your goddamn *partner*." Stoney stepped over him like he was a pile of dog shit. "If you'll excuse me, Ty. I got work to do. Horses need worming."

His eyes were watering, and Ford tasted blood in his mouth, but he had to admit, he admired Stoney for having the balls to do it. He glanced at Ty.

Ty arched one eyebrow, shook his head. "Texans. Still, never seen anyone piss him off like that. No one but you."

"Yeah, well, good for me." He climbed up off the floor. "Good thing I canceled all my meetings for the next week."

"Yeah, you're gonna bruise." Ty didn't seem concerned about it, one way or the other.

"I never said he was a drunk, by the way. I said he was busy playing drunk cowboy. Thanks for tossing me under the bus."

Ty pinned him with a glare. "You have how many degrees? I expect you to be the one I can reason with, you butthead."

"I'm trying to be reasonable. He's a fucker."

"Grandpa! They're stealing your dresser!" Quartz pelted in and grabbed Ty's hands. "Stop them!"

"Oh, Quartz, boy, I'm moving to the Junction. Remember?"

"No. No, you live here! You stay here!" Quartz looked fierce, fists balled up tight.

"I can't, buddy. I'm real sick."

"No! No! You live here with me and Daddy!"

Ty's face screwed up, and Ford hated that his uncle was sick. Hated it so bad for a moment that he wanted to throw his own tantrum. Instead, he slipped out and grabbed his phone, texting Stoney.

Quartz and Ty need you.
On my way.

He heard the clack of bootheels on the tile floor in mere minutes. "Quartz? Son?"

"Daddy! No. Tell Grandpa he has to stay!"

"Oh, son...." Stoney sighed, and Ford braced himself for another cold response, but what he heard was "I know it hurts, but Grampa has to go. He's going to come visit, and you'll be able to go there. He's going to miss you, so bad. It's going to be weird, but I need you here with me, because Grampa's got Miss Sophia."

"I don't want him to go." Quartz was sniffling, though, not screaming.

"No, but Miss Sophia is waiting for him."

"Will she bring him for supper sometimes?"

"Ask him, bud," Stoney said.

Ford faded back, not wanting to eavesdrop now that the storm seemed averted. He checked on the status of Ty's move, looking at the bed with a critical eye. Lodgepole pine, strong and sturdy. He'd need a new mattress and box springs, but he could get those tomorrow in Glenwood.

He rubbed his jaw, wincing at the swollen heat and soreness. Little bastard could hit. He needed to find him some Advil or something.

Ty's words made him grin, though. Never seen anyone make Stoney that mad but him? Shit. Wait until Stoney saw what Ford intended to do with the ranch.

He might have to wear a helmet for that one.

Ty finally joined him in the big master bedroom, looking a bit gray. "Lord. I forget how they are at that age."

"I'm sorry." He clapped Ty gently on the shoulder. This had to be the hardest thing the old man had done, save dealing with Brit dying on him and his wife leaving him less than a year later. "You need me to drive you back to Grand Junction? I can bring one of the hands to drive your truck."

"No, sir. I'm fine. I'm going to get on, though. The boys know what else to bring of mine. All the rest is yours to do with as you see fit."

"Holler when you get home so we know." He surprised himself by taking a hug.

"I love you, son. Please try to get along with Stoney, huh? You two can do this. I know it."

"Hey, I've asked for meetings and tried to give him his space. He has to get to halfway." Ford held up both hands when Ty scowled. "I'll try, okay? I promise."

"Good man. I appreciate it. I've got to go, huh? I can't leave if he comes back in."

"Okay." Ford walked Ty to the door, checking to make sure Ty was steady enough to drive. DeBeque Canyon could be a bear.

"You'll keep an eye on Quartz for me? I know Stoney has to take the hunting trips for days at a time and that little girl watches him, but…."

"I will." Whoa. How weird was that request? Still, he'd do it because Ty asked.

"Thank you." Ty patted his arm, then looked back at the ranch house with a sigh and headed for his truck.

Ford remembered how that had hurt when he left for college. He could only imagine how Ty felt. He shook his head and made his way to the kitchen, needing a cup of coffee. Badly.

"Can we please have something Quartz-friendly for staff supper, man? If you already have plans, I'll feed him myself. He's on a tear."

Eavesdropping again. Ford brazened it out, stepping into the kitchen. "Is there anything I can do?"

Stoney shot him a look. "I reckon you've done enough." The "asshole" was silent, but still right there. "You missed our seven o'clock. When you thinking on rescheduling?"

The madder Stoney was, the more hick he sounded.

Ford crossed his arms over his chest, then made himself drop the defensive pose. "Depends on how many worms the horses have, I suppose."

"You're more than welcome to stick an arm up their asses to check, boss."

Geoff's eyes were the size of dinner plates.

"Not your boss. You said it yourself. So one can only assume you're using that in a derogatory way. My name is Ford, as you well know." He kept his tone even and worked hard not to sound as if he was speaking to a small child. Damn it, Stoney was the most stubborn, determined-to-do-things-the-hard-way asshole Ford had ever met.

"My bad. You're more than welcome to stick an arm up their asses to check, *pardner*. Text me when you want to chat."

"How about after lunch?" He glanced at Geoff. "Do we have cereal?"

"Chex, Cheerios, Frosted Flakes, Apple Jacks, and Frosted Mini Wheats. Take your pick."

"We good for supper, Geoff?" Geoff nodded and Stoney did too. "I'll be in the office at one. I got to settle in a guy that's taking cabin three for a week. Geoff, he'll eat with the family in cabin one and the *artiste* in cabin eight."

"Got it." Geoff grabbed a marker and scribbled on the big white board behind the pantry door. Nice to see someone was organized.

"One it is," Ford said, and grabbed the Chex. He had a lot to do.

He had a whole half of a house to decorate and a business plan to lay out so even a redneck Texas college dropout could understand it.

He also really needed to work on his ducking skills.

Chapter Twelve

STONEY swore by all he held holy, if one more person texted him with an emergency this morning….

Between Ty's shitty timing, Ford's lies, the exploding water heater in cabin four, and Quartz's meltdown, Stoney was going to kill something.

"I'm sorry, boss." Alanna sniffled, cheek bright red. "I…. He…."

"He knows better, and he's damn lucky I don't take him behind the house and whip his ass!" Stoney made sure Quartz heard him. He'd never spanked the boy in anger in his whole life, but the threat seemed to be a fine deterrent, and he'd be damned if he raised a son that hit a girl.

"I didn't mean to!"

"Didn't mean to throw the fucking book and pop Miss Alanna in the face? How exactly do you do that by accident? Seriously, educate me. I'm dying to hear this."

"Daddy!" Quartz had that look. The one that said meltdown, but Stoney wasn't having it.

"Alanna, can you give us a minute?"

"Absolutely. I'm going to grab a bite for lunch, okay?"

"Totally. You'll come back to a body or an apology, one or the other."

She chuckled, but stifled it fast. Yeah. This had to be serious.

Quartz sighed, shoulders hunching. "I didn't mean to hit her."

"What did I tell you about throwing things?"

"Not to."

"And you did it anyway."

"I was mad!" Quartz shouted.

"I don't give a shit how mad you are, you don't get to throw things at girls. You want to fight with someone, you come fight with me."

"I wouldn't fight with you, Daddy! You're bigger than me!"

"The best thing is not to fight at all." Unless you were talking about that fuck monkey Ford. That was a fight more than ten years in the making, and it had felt like heaven to pop that motherfucker in the face. What? Stoney didn't have to be fair. This was a do as I say, not as I do situation.

"I was so mad." Quartz's lip began to quiver. "Why does Grandpa have to go?"

"Because he's sick and the dialysis is there. If he doesn't get treatment, he will die, no question. He wants you to come for some time before Christmas and this summer." It wasn't as if he hadn't explained this, over and over.

"I hate that he's sick, Daddy. I don't want Uncle Ford. I want Grandpa."

"I hate that he's sick too, but there's nothing we can do about that. All living things have to die, and this is a part of that."

"Why?"

"It's God's way." It was a pat answer, but it was the one he understood.

"I hate God sometimes."

"Me too." At Quartz's surprised look, Stoney shrugged. "What? I ain't perfect, boy. I'm just a cowboy getting along best I can. Sometimes my heart is so mad at things I cain't hardly bear it."

"So what do you do, Daddy?"

"You have faith, son. You have faith that there's a plan that's bigger than us."

Quartz came to him, grabbed him tight and squeezed. "I love you, Daddy. I'm so tired in my heart."

"Yessir. Me too. Tired to stupidity." He petted Quartz's curly dark hair. "Still, we got each other, you and me, and we got this whole thing, right?"

"We have horses." Quartz brightened at that. "Can we go ride?"

"No, sir. Not until we think about what you're going to do to make up to Miss Alanna."

"Yeah. I was bad. I'll draw her a picture, and then I'll be the best for my lessons this afternoon, okay?"

"I think that's a good start, son." Thank God for a boy who was basically a good'un.

"Then maybe we can ride after your meeting?"

"We'll see what Miss Alanna says, I guess."

"Yes, sir."

"Good boy. You want to make peanut butter sandwiches with me for lunch?"

"I do!" Quartz could be distracted by peanut butter in almost any situation. Stoney used it without shame.

By the time sandwiches were eaten, Alanna was back, and Quartz was all over himself apologizing.

"Thank you, Quartz. Geoff sent you an oatmeal Scotchie."

"Oh. Can I have it, Daddy?"

"Have it for your snack, huh? Before we ride?"

"Yessir." Quartz hugged him, clearly ready to move on.

"I got to hustle, y'all. Have a better afternoon."

"We will, boss. Thank you." Alanna closed the door behind him so he could concentrate on steeling himself for Ford.

Okay, he would not hit the son of a bitch. He would just stand there, listen, and leave. No temper tantrums. He wasn't nine like his kid.

Ford got his goat, for sure.

Still, telling Ty he was a drunk. Shit. The man deserved it.

Stoney took a deep breath before he knocked on the door to Ty's office. Which was Ford's now.

"Come on!" Ford said.

The urge to snarl "yes, boss" was huge, but Ford was right in that. He wasn't anyone's employee. So he ducked inside, noting that Ford had cleaned off the extra chair, the files stacked on the floor instead.

"Have a seat." He hesitated, and Ford sighed. "Come on, seriously. Shut the door and take a chair so we can talk."

The man sported what was going to be one hell of a bruise in the morning. The sight gave Stoney a tiny spurt of happy.

Ford swiveled to face Stoney, his long-sleeved T-shirt and faded jeans a surprise. Not buttoned up at all.

Interesting.

He sat, his back creaking and popping all the way down.

"Long morning?" Ford didn't sound sarcastic or mean, so Stoney figured the question was polite interest.

"Yes, sir. I've had better."

"Me too." Ford rubbed his bruised face. "Look, I owe you an apology. I should never have told Ty you were a drunk."

"You're right. You shouldn't have. I wasn't even a heavy drinker back in school." That had come out of left field and made him so mad he'd seen red.

"Every time I see you, you look hung over. You don't eat either. I just figured you were hitting the sauce."

What was he supposed to say? He worked hard, long hours, and he was tired.

Ford shrugged. "Whatever I thought, I was wrong. So I'm sorry."

"Apology accepted." Stoney could forgive some things. He was a good guy, right?

"Good, because we have a good bit to talk about." Ford turned back to the computer to call up a program.

Yippee.

He leaned back and waited. That he knew how to do.

"Okay, so in order to renew the BLM, I had to put in an updated land-use plan."

He knew that. He'd written up one that had been rejected already.

"I put in for horses, including the mustangs, since Ty says that's your real love, as well as hunting, as I know that pays bills." Ford highlighted shit on a pie chart.

He nodded. It wasn't his favorite job, but it paid.

"This is fallow land that we agree to rotate."

"I'm all for land I don't have to stress over."

"Right, because the rest is going to cause you stress." Ford clicked on the biggest piece of the pie.

He forced himself not to change expressions, to stay stony, pun intended.

"You ready?" Ford gave him a sideways look, a half grin that made him work hard not to smile back.

"I was born ready." Ready and tired.

"Well, I think the ranch has a real shot at being a sort of… retreat. An event destination. That's a real catchword right now. Destination vacations, destination weddings."

He had to give Ford an incredulous look. Had to. *Seriously? Here? An event destination?* They couldn't fucking book the redneckiest wedding party ever. The periodic photo hunt? Sure. But a destination?

Shit.

"What? We're close to Glenwood and Aspen. The airport in Junction has more direct flights now than ever. People want authentic ranch experiences mixed with glamping." Ford warmed visibly to the subject.

Glamping?
Did Ford just say glamping?
Seriously?

"Does it speak, or do you have to wind it up first?"

"Don't make me hit you." *Again.*

"I never make anyone do anything." Ford brought up another spreadsheet. "This is the market share of resort vacations for Glenwood Hot Springs. Then there's a couple of dude ranches in the Roaring Fork."

"We're not a dude ranch." Hell, he had to fight Ty to run as many horses as he did.

"No, but we could really work the riding angle. Photographers, weddings, team building. I think you could do way more with the riding horses than you do, really expand that part of the operation. Maybe see what Hetty is willing to do with wagons and hayrides with her Belgians." Ford spread his hands. "Hunting is still good for the ecosystem, but it's become a rich man's game too. We can cater to the guys with more to spend but focus on ethical hunting so no one gets their nose out of joint."

"What does that mean, for real?" Stoney followed all the rules, religiously, and stewardship was important to him. The good Lord trusted them with this land; it was on them to care for it.

"In cowboy terms, it means a lot of folks these days, including a few of the BLM managers, are falling out of love with guided hunts. Let's face it, hunters get better weather and more chances at big bucks in Texas, where they can get up close." Ford paused, head tilting like it always had when he was thinking hard. "It means I think we can really do better business by being utterly unique in this area."

Right, because he was unique. Christ, how was he supposed to fit into this mess?

"I'm happy to let them loose, so long as we're not held responsible for when someone fucks up."

"Are we speaking the same language?" Ford wasn't growling or anything. More seeming confused.

"I doubt it. I lead all the hunting parties around here, you know?"

"Right. You still would. I'm just saying that there's this perception that guided hunts lead hunters to within ten feet of an elk, aim the gun, and let the guy pull the trigger." Ford held up a hand. "I know better, but we have to distinguish ourselves from those outfits."

"I'm fine with that." That wasn't cool. If you wanted to hunt that way…. Shit, he didn't even have a *then* for that thought.

Ford nodded, his face relaxing. "Well, brace yourself. I want to do some advertising."

"I'd chat with Miranda about that. She's in charge of all the web and ad stuff along with the office." He dealt with guests and horses and staff. That was his job, and he sort of loved it.

"Okay. Thing is, you need to know what I'm advertising. I want us to be inclusive, so I want to advertise in some gay magazines and newspapers." Ford waited, expression carefully smooth.

"Is there a huge market for gay hunters?" That would be unexpected and more than a little hilarious. Not only that, but someone not him was going to have to tell Ty.

"Hell if I know. I mean as a wedding and retreat place. Geoff would bring them back year after year, and your horses would get all the work they need." Ford chuckled, though, snorting a bit.

"Uh-huh, right. Look, I don't want to be Debbie Downer, but you're a rich gay guy, and you wouldn't pay to come here, and it's your family home."

"I didn't come home because you were here." Ford sighed, a look of exaggerated patience on his face. "I was right. You hit me."

Was Ford teasing him? Seriously. He searched Ford's face, seeing nothing but laughter.

"And you didn't even duck. That's prob'ly a sign of deserving it."

Ford snorted, green eyes dancing. "I figured you could have one after all these years."

"Uh-huh. You're going to bruise like a motherfucker. You'll have to tell everybody you ran into a hoof."

"Nope. I'll tell them I have an abusive partner, and everyone will feel sorry for me."

"Possibly. You never know with cowboys." Angie was going to ride Ford's ass for days.

"All of the cowboys know what really happened by now," Ford said with absolute conviction. "No one will feel bad for me there."

He had nothing to say about that. It was true. Ford had deserved an ass whipping for telling lies.

"So, are you willing to work with me on the concept? You seem pretty open."

"I don't see that anyone's going to come here for some sort of fancy deal, but you want to put feelers out, go for it." It wouldn't change a thing about his life. Fancy-assed assholes—queer or not—wouldn't show up to a place like this.

"Okay, cool. So, now we need to talk about accommodations." Ford pulled up a budget chart. Holy shit, that was a lot of money.

"What's all that for?" And where the fuck was it coming from?

"I want to renovate cabins three and four pretty extensively. I want to build two new cabins. The rest is for minor fixes, and then I want to take the old greenhouse and storage barn and turn it into an event building for receptions and meetings and such." Ford was practically bouncing, clearly super excited.

Who is this guy?

Stoney shook his head. "How can we afford that? We're running at thirty percent occupancy on good months. I ain't laying folks off, man. No way."

"You don't need to. In fact, I project we'll need two new housekeeping staff, a general assistant and two more part-time wranglers for trail rides and such. Geoff might need an assistant for off-site meals, as well. A camp cook."

Just like that? Right.

"Where's the money coming from?" Seriously. Stoney made payroll and his vet bills, but even the horse feed came out of his salary.

"I'll be making the initial investment." Ford held up a hand. "You know I do contract law, Stoney. I won't fuck you on this, and if we make a profit, we'll both share in it. Ty had every right to ask me for help over the years, and he didn't. It's my turn to put in some principal."

So what? Ford was going to come in here and make this place the going thing because obviously he couldn't? Christ on a crutch. Stoney hated this—hated having the rug pulled out from under him, over and over again in the place that was supposed to be home.

"You're pissed. I can tell." Ford sat back in the big desk chair, hands steepled in front of him, watching Stoney carefully. That's what Ford did. Watched and waited and gauged reactions. Then he freaked out and ran after it was all over. Stoney reckoned it was the first half that made him a good lawyer.

Good thing one of the things that made Stoney a cowboy was the ability to sit still and just let the world pass him by. That he had down to a science.

"Come on, Stoney. Talk to me. Just once in your life, say something out fucking loud."

"I feel like y'all are planning shit to phase me out."

"Y'all who? Ty?" Ford raised an eyebrow. "Trust me. He's not sharing his plans with me either."

Yeah, right. Because everyone just came up with a plan like this out of the blue. The thought that maybe everyone else did snuck in before he even opened his mouth. Maybe other people could just fix things. "Well, I'm sorry you got stuck working with me."

He had Quartz, though, and he couldn't just walk away.

"Stoney, I need you to stop. Right there. Stop acting like you've given up and are ready to fail. We can make this place somewhere Ty and Quartz can both count on to support them. I know we can."

"I haven't given up on dick. I've been working my ass off for the last ten years."

"Then why are you sitting there with your teeth in your mouth looking like you lost your last horse? I liked it better when you were hitting me." Ford grimaced, and Stoney almost knocked him winding.

"Sorry. I just…." Shit, he didn't fucking know what the hell was up with the whole motherfucking world.

"Okay." Ford reached out and touched his shoulder, and he'd be damned if electricity didn't shoot down his arm, just like the first time they'd ever met. "Okay, you're right. I need to give you time to process everything."

"Yeah. I'm going to get some work done, blow some dust out, you know?"

"Sure."

He wanted to scream, to ask if Ford had hit his head when he fell. What was going on here?

A gay destination resort? All this shit? Stoney just....

God, he wanted to go home. Except this was the only place he knew to call that anymore, and he couldn't even breathe here.

He stood up and headed out the door, going straight for the barns and the horses that were waiting for him. They always needed care, and they always made sense.

Ford, he didn't get at all.

Chapter Thirteen

STONEY avoided Ford for damned near a week.

He let it happen because, to be fair, Stoney had a lot to process. Ford was trying to do what Ty asked and give the guy space and all, but damn. Winter was hard upon them, and Thanksgiving was coming, and….

"Shit." Ford rose, grabbed his coat on the way out the back, and waded into the newest crust of snow.

He could hear hammering coming from the back of one of the cabins, could hear Stoney singing along with George Strait.

Ford had to grin. You could take the boy out of Texas. He peered around the cabin, hunting said Texan.

Stoney was fixing shingles, all alone. Crazy son of a bitch. Why on earth wasn't Stoney doing something important and hiring someone to do this menial upkeep?

"Hey! What the hell are you doing, man?" Ford shaded his eyes and stared up at the roof.

"Fixing shingles."

Yes, he could see that. Christ, if Stoney strung more than three words together in a row, he'd be stunned.

"Why are you doing this and not a maintenance man?"

"Not been one here since the spring."

"Why not?" If he could get his hands on a hammer, he would hit Stoney. Hard.

"Victor quit."

Irritating motherfucker. Ford closed his eyes, counting to ten. "I'm trying here, Stoney. You could meet me halfway."

Stoney stopped hammering, then took a deep breath. "Victor left in a snit, and there's nothing I can't fix, for the most part, and I figured we'd save a few pennies. That's all."

"Okay. I'll work a handyman into the budget. I need to sit and talk to you about operations. We got Thanksgiving and Christmas, and I have no idea how any of that works."

Stoney blinked down at him, obviously confused. "Well, Thanksgiving is turkey and Christmas is Santa and lights. Usually there's a ham."

"I bet there's also tofu loaf, knowing Geoff. What I want to know is, are there guests? Will Ty come in? What should I get Quartz?"

Stoney's laugh rang out, and Ford found himself blinking up, stunned into silence by the unexpected sound. "Tofurky shit. Avoid it like the plague. We got one family looking to unplug their teenagers, I think, between Thanksgiving and Christmas, but it ain't a big time for hunters. I'm getting Quartz a tablet, so maybe a gift card for games would be nice."

Hello! Ford had found the push button. Woo. So, now would not be the best time to mention a Christmas open house. Mainly Ford wanted to invite contractors and community business people, help make some connections for all the work they needed to do in the spring.

He wanted the place decorated up nice too, so there could be pictures for the website.

"Cool. Games I can do. My assistant in Santa Fe is a huge geek." God, he hadn't been home in… weeks. Christ. Really? Eileen was going to rip off his head and shit down his neck.

Also, he'd obviously been spending too much time with cowboys.

"Yeah, me not so much, but Quartz loves making things."

"I'll have to consult him on my tech." Ford was glad he was wearing his treaded boots. He glanced around for the inevitable toolbox.

"What you need, man?"

"A hammer." He could help out and get the job done that much faster.

"There's one up here…."

"Come on, Stoney. I grew up here. I know how to lay shingles." Not to mention he worked with Habitat for Humanity every summer. Ford climbed the ladder, holding out a hand for a hammer.

Stoney handed it over. "Thanks, man."

Okay. Okay, that was actually pleasant.

Ford grinned, feeling like he was actually helping out for the first time since the BLM contract. It was a good thing. They worked together and got the roof repaired, but by the time they were done, Ford was frozen, and he could only guess how cold Stoney had to be.

"Geoff probably has coffee," Stoney said.

"Probably? That man is a coffee whore."

"True. He also keeps mulled cider in a crock pot."

"What the hell are we doing up here on the roof, then?" Were they having a conversation? Him and Stoney?

"Fixing the roof, Ford."

"Yeah, well, it's fixed. I say we find cookies."

"Cool." Stoney put the tools away as he headed down the ladder, then shimmied down himself, giving him a look at a tight little ass.

Ford couldn't help but look. He'd always admired that butt. It had been fine in college, but now it looked hard and firm enough to bounce a quarter off.

The things he could do with that….

Only not so much.

Stoney was… what? Bi? Why Brit? Why jump from him to his cousin? He didn't get it. Hell, maybe Stoney had been experimenting with him, but the way he'd sucked…. Well, a man had to be into cock for that.

"You okay, man?"

"Yeah. Sorry. I could murder some lunch."

"Head on in. I'll put stuff away."

Ford paused, then decided to trust. "See you inside."

Stoney trundled into the maintenance shed, the wind blowing the door open as a new round of snow began to fall.

Lord, it was cold. The ski places ought to be ecstatic this year. Maybe they should have some cross-country trails, training. Snowshoes.

"Huh. Mental note." He stomped snow off his boots at the back door, then almost fell over when Geoff opened it.

"About what?"

"Snowshoes."

"Ah. Love them. You?"

"Went once." He shrugged. "I'll try it again."

"Cool. You looking for anything in particular?"

"Lunch." He chuckled. "Frozen."

"Ah. I have vegetarian chili and grilled cheese."

Oh, that sounded magical. "Enough for Stoney too?"

"Of course. Everybody else ate while the boss was playing the martyr."

"Well, I helped him out." His hands felt like hamburger. "I'll wash up if you can show me where to dish out."

"Bowls. Spoons. I'll make sandwiches."

"I'm on it." Ford ran water as hot as he could stand it and scrubbed.

He saw Stoney tromping across the yard, and he was only stopped, what? Ten times on the way? Everyone wanted a piece of the guy, which was why he shouldn't be on the roof fixing shingles.

That wasn't a good use of Stoney's skills, dammit.

"You're looking all grim," Stoney told Ford when he walked inside.

"Nah, this is determination."

"Ah. Good to know." Little shit.

Ford pulled out bowls and spoons. "Geoff is making sammies."

"Cool." Stoney headed for the sink. "There coffee?"

Geoff rolled his eyes. "Duh."

Ford chuckled. "Okay, here's a question you'll like. What kind do we have today?"

"Pinyon from down your way. I love it. It smells like chocolate."

"It does. I should bring up a load of wood next time I come up. It makes the whole house smell amazing."

"Ty likes that, quite a bit." Stoney washed his hands, the skin raw and red.

He frowned. Gloves. Someone needed work gloves for Christmas. "Yeah? You think he'll come in for the holidays?"

"Miss Sophia wants to visit her kids in Vermont, so I don't know. He'll be here for one of them, I'm sure."

"Wow." Ford just—he felt both out of the loop and a little hurt. He and Ty hadn't spent the holidays together since he'd left home, and while Ford knew that was his fault, he'd still been looking forward to the idea this year.

"Yeah. They're having fights, from what Quartz says. None of mine."

"Right." Ford chuckled. "I guess it's tough to blend lives at their age."

Geoff laughed. "Dude! My Aunt Louise retired as a nun and married a lady up in British Columbia ten years ago. You want to talk about adjustment."

"I bet. There she had to divorce Jesus."

He blinked at Stoney. When had the Cowboy of Stone developed a sense of humor?

Geoff cracked up and slid two sandwiches onto plates. "Yessir. And she had to eat weird Canadian food."

"Hey, I eat your weird-assed vegetarian chili, don't I?"

"It's good." Geoff looked all offended for the two seconds he kept a straight face.

Stoney nodded and gave Geoff an easy, relaxed hug. "It is. I'd even admit to eating it."

"There, see?"

The red hot flash of jealousy Ford felt spear through him shocked him, jolting him to his toes. He didn't want Stoney touching someone else.

He wanted that easy grin directed at him, dammit. Ford was trying. He really was. Working with Stoney instead of against him. This bizarre wave of homesickness hit him, because even though he was back at the ranch, he knew in his heart no one wanted him there.

Still.

"You okay, man?" Stoney asked, and the offhand kindness was almost too much to bear.

"I'm fine." Ford didn't force a smile, because it would just be obvious. "Just need to eat, I think." He sat at the kitchen table, because the big table was too formal.

Stoney settled next to him, eating like a man who was starving. Skinny butt. He needed to eat more.

"You okay if I run to Carbondale for supplies, boss?" Geoff asked.

"Totally. Grab me some apples, would you?"

"You got it. Anything for you, other boss?" Geoff gyrated a brow at him.

"Swiss Cake Rolls."

"Those things are obscene."

"Oh, man…." Stoney leaned in, close enough that he could see the flecks of silver in Stoney's eyes. "Just nod or he'll be inventing his own for days."

"Mmm. Okay. I mean, I need something sweet and gross. I know you like salty and crunchy, but I'm having stress."

"Get him the Little Debbies, and I'll let you make tofu this week, Geoff."

"I'll make it crispy!" Geoff bounced out, bellowing what sounded like *Don Giovanni*.

"Thanks." He nudged Stoney with his elbow. "This chili is good."

"Yeah. He's a damn good cook. I found him at the bus station beat half to death trying to get out of town."

"What? What happened?" Christ. Geoff didn't seem confrontational at all, and he was Desiree's brother, for fuck's sake.

"He was here visiting family. They're sort of the hippie-dippie types. You know, Quonset huts on the river. His sister, Desiree, was one of Brit's friends. Apparently some assholes took offense to the fact he was gay and beat the living fuck out of him. I was picking up a couple of wranglers, and there he was. I couldn't leave him there. He needed a safe place, and I had one."

"You're a good man, Stoney." The words popped out, but Ford found he meant them. He'd seen Stoney with Quartz, with Ty, with all the staff.

Hell, the man was even being nice to Ford right now.

"Why did you hook up with Britney, Stoney?" Oh, fuck. There it was.

"What?" Why the fuck did Stoney look confused?

"I mean—" Ford waved a hand in the air. "Why didn't you just tell me you were bi? Was that why you…." He trailed off, not sure why he had diarrhea of the mouth.

"What the fuck are you on about? Are you trying to prove a point or something?" Stoney gave him a scowl, thunderclouds brewing.

"Prove a point? About what? You knocked up my cousin? I want to know why! I mean, I was pretty sure you were full-on queer back in the day!"

"I didn't…." Stoney cut himself off so quickly Ford swore he could hear it. Then the son of a bitch just stood and left. Just walked off without another fucking word, leaving what was left of his food behind.

Stoney didn't? Stoney didn't *what*?

Ford hopped up and chased Stoney outside. "No. I want to know!" He slammed into Stoney's shoulder like a defensive lineman, sending them both sprawling. "How the fuck could you do it?"

"Do what? Save her ass? Save Ty's? I did it. This is my home, you motherfucker!"

"What does that even mean?" Ford slogged his way to his feet, panting from the shock of the cold mud.

"What part don't you understand? I did what I had to, and I don't regret it. She wasn't supposed to die on the river. It wasn't supposed to be…." Stoney threw up his hands and then stood, cold mud dripping from him.

"You had to get my cousin pregnant? That doesn't make any fucking sense!"

Stoney looked at him like he'd lost his mind, but he knew he hadn't. He *knew* it.

"What? What the hell is it I don't understand? How is getting her knocked up covering her ass?" Ford was going to blow a vein.

"We're not talking about this here," Stoney hissed. "Anyone could hear us."

"Then come back and talk to me, damn it. Stop running away." Ford held out a hand. "Make me understand."

"I thought you already did." It took a second, but Stoney accepted his offer, rough calluses dragging against his skin.

"I don't get anything that's going on around here." They headed inside, and Ford shivered. Man, they needed towels.

He took Stoney into his part of the house, back past the office and the little family room and into the room he was using as a sitting room-slash-library.

"Let me grab some towels and that Thermos of coffee Geoff always leaves me."

"Yeah, sure."

He hurried to the bathroom, stripping off his soaking sweater; he grabbed him some sweats, his robe, and a handful of towels. To his utter surprise, Stoney was still there when he got back, staring at the books piled on the shelf beside his desk.

"You're welcome to borrow any of them you'd like."

Stoney damn near jumped out of his skin. "No. No, that's cool."

"I know you read, Stoney. It's not like I think you're stupid." He didn't. Stoney thought that for him, always putting himself down.

"Towel? I'm dripping on your floor."

"Here." He handed over a towel and his robe. He had sweats to slip into, and he'd forgotten Stoney would be freezing as well as wet.

"It's okay. I'd just get it nasty." Stoney tried to dry off, then sighed. "I should go change."

"Promise you'll come right back?" They lived in the same house. He couldn't hold Stoney hostage.

"Where am I going to go?" The hopelessness in the words surprised him, but Stoney just shrugged. "I'll be back in a minute."

The slump of Stoney's shoulders spoke of defeat, and Ford wondered if he'd stepped aside into another dimension. "Look, you stubborn bastard. Just tell me what happened with you and Brittany. Why did you sleep with her?"

"I didn't."

"What?" Ford felt as though someone had hit him in the gut. "But Quartz is your kid."

"He's my son. My name's on the birth certificate, and I'll beat anyone down who says otherwise."

"Please tell me, Stoney." He gave Stoney the robe, and this time the man took it and slid out of his shirt and hoodie before putting it on.

"She caught pregnant from a guy in Aspen, someone important enough and married enough that Ty worried, I guess. He came to me and asked if I'd put my name on the birth certificate, say it was mine so's she wouldn't get in trouble. She wasn't supposed to die."

Ford felt an increasingly familiar sensation of being hit, right in the breadbasket.

"I—how." He sat in the chair that was, thankfully, right behind him. Ford spread his hands. "Why wouldn't someone tell me that?"

"I thought you knew."

"Clearly not." Fuck. All this time he'd hated Stoney for not just taking his home, but moving on so damned fast. With his cousin. The floor was just—shit, it was just gone like a black hole opened up under him and he was free-falling in space.

"She wasn't supposed to die. I mean, he was just a baby, and… I love him. I couldn't turn away from him, not for anything."

"No. No, of course not." Ford wanted to scream. He wanted to call Ty and read the old bastard the riot act. "I couldn't understand it, man. I just couldn't. Jesus, I wanted to know why so bad, and now there isn't a why."

"Ford, man, I left you because I'm a fucking idiot, not because I decided to stop being gay."

Ford stared at Stoney, not sure what to say at all. He was never lost for words.

"Quartz is my life now. You won't tell him." It wasn't a question.

"I'm not a complete dick." Even if his whole family clearly thought he was. Christ. He could have helped. What had Ty thought of him? What kind of bastard did Ty think he was, for fuck's sake?

"No. I'm not either."

No. No, in fact, Stoney was a good guy. Like a genuinely decent human being. Ford couldn't even argue Stoney had done what he had to get the ranch. No one had expected Brit to frickin' drown.

Ford kind of wanted to kick him in the shins. Not hard enough to bruise, just enough to make it sting. Or maybe beat that still fine ass until it was raw.

"I wish Ty had told me. I could have helped."

"I thought he had."

"Yes, well, you should have verified."

One eyebrow shot up. "Sure. Dear guy who hates me. You did know that I didn't fuck your cousin because I'm, one, queer as a three-dollar bill, and two, not a giant bleeding asshole, right? Also, there's the baby that doesn't look anything like me situation and the fact that I agreed to take half the ranch to give Quartz something I couldn't manage on my own. Your former lover, the total loser."

Okay, that was the longest speech from Stoney ever.

It was also bullshit. Ford wouldn't have turned away from Brit back then, even if he was mad at Stoney and Ty. "I would have done something, Stoney. I would have. Hell, I stayed away because I thought every damned member of this family thought I was an utter prick, when it comes right down to it."

"You know Ty loves you."

"You don't have to like someone to love them." He sighed, studying Stoney's face, trying to find something familiar in this stranger. "I'm sorry. I promise, we'll make the ranch into something Quartz can count on for college money or whatever he wants to do."

"He wants to be an engineer. He wants to build huge things." Stoney smiled as he said the words, the obvious love the man had for his son enough to make Ford forgive a lot. Stoney could have walked away, could have let Brit and Ty hang, but he hadn't. Far from it.

Some small part of that may have been that Stoney didn't know what else to do, but that wasn't the only reason, clearly. It also wasn't Ford's place to judge.

Fuck, his head hurt.

"That's too cool," Ford said. "Has he ever been to science camp?"

"Do they have those?"

God save him from insular cowboys with gorgeous gray eyes and perfect asses. Ford rolled his eyes. "Yes. And God knows, he could use some time with kids more like him. That was not a criticism," Ford added, holding up a hand to stall the protest obviously forming.

"Yeah, it sorta is, and I sorta deserve it. It's hard to let him go do things. I worry."

"Like, in general, or does he have specific issues?" Ford needed to know everything. Now.

"He's got autism. He's doing great, compared to a few years ago, but he's got himself his momma's temper and…." Stoney shrugged. "He has to try harder than other kids, but he's wicked smart and just about the neatest person I've ever met."

"He's honest as hell, which I like." Ford rolled his head on his neck. "Sorry about tackling you. I'm glad you told me, though." He could stop thinking the worst of Brittany too, which relieved his mind. Maybe he was a shitty human being. Who knew?

"I really thought you knew. Honest. Not many folks know, but I thought you were one of them." Stoney held out one hand to him.

Ford took it, half shaking, half just holding. The gesture felt a lot like Stoney handing him a lifeline. The calluses fascinated his thumb, and he found himself exploring them, one hard ridge after another.

Stoney stared at him, lips open the tiniest bit, cheeks flushed. Oh, God, he wanted—

Ford let Stoney's hand loose. "You need to go take a hot shower, man."

"Yeah. I'll wash your robe." Stoney headed out, damn near running.

Ford found himself grinning, even in the mood he was in.

Possibly because he'd heard Stoney mutter, "Hot shower, my ass. I need a cold one."

Chapter Fourteen

"WHY didn't you tell him, Ty?" Stoney knew Ty would be awake early, and he wanted to get this talk out on the table so he could get on with his day.

"What's that, son?" Ty asked, coughing roughly on the last word.

Stoney winced, but he couldn't let this go. "About Quartz. You didn't tell him."

Ty remained silent so long Stoney wondered if he'd fallen asleep. Then Ty drew a deep breath. "He didn't come to Brit's funeral."

"You had two years before that, give or take." The truth really seemed to have set Ford free. If Ford had known, would he have come home?

"I wanted to. I did. You know I was afraid to call for a bit after I took you on, and then he wouldn't even come—" Ty coughed harder. "Shit. Sophia!"

"Okay. It's okay, old man." He waited for Ty to come back, hoping all was well.

"Sorry, boy."

"It's fine. We'll talk later." Stoney knew they wouldn't. The simple truth was, Ty was dying, and his motives didn't matter as much as him enjoying what time he had left. "I love you. Quartz wants to come down for a weekend."

"You bet. You just say."

"Maybe next weekend."

"Sophia is off then, so that would be perfect."

"Well, I'll bring him down." He sighed. "Love you, old man," he repeated.

"Love you, Stoney. You can do this." Ty sounded so sure.

The thing was, Stoney was really beginning to think so too.

Chapter Fifteen

"**FORD!** Glad you could make it." Matt Gregson stood, waving Ford over to the table at the restaurant, a sweet little Italian place with family-style service. The twins were there, still amazing and beautiful, and there were some new faces Ford didn't recognize from high school.

This was some sort of business leads club, where they all sat around and networked. Ford thought that was a great way to get the new concept of the ranch out there, to make some allies.

"Me too." Ford shook hands all around. He introduced himself to two guys who worked in advertising, one in Aspen and one in Basalt. Nice.

"I owe you one for the coffee," Matt said. "What would you like to drink?"

"I think I'd like a glass of red, Chianti if it's available."

"Oh, the hard-core wine. Come on, let's go up to the bar. They'll bring out a fixed series of appetizers for us, but we deal with our own drinks."

"Sure." He followed Matt to the bar. "How's Sharon?" He hoped he got her name right. Ford felt totally distracted. All he could think about was Stoney.

"Pregnant." Matt winked and Ford had to grin.

"Better you than me, Matt."

"Yes, well." Matt shot him this smartassed look that was all waggling eyebrows and twinkling eyes. "Some of us are having to reproduce for all you boys."

"Go you and your amazing het loins." He had to smile when Matt hooted, drawing stares.

"Ford? Ford Nixel? When did you get back in town?"

He glanced over and raised his eyebrows. "Andy? Hey, man, how are you?" Wow. Andy looked sleek as an otter, his expensive coat and designer boots all perfectly matching.

"I'm fabulous! Been busy keeping my clients happy. Are you back in Aspen for a while?"

"Just stopping in for supper." He didn't know why he was being so cagey. Andy was an ex, one with whom Ford had spent two years trying to work it out, and he just didn't want to share too much of what was going on. Andy hadn't been interested in living half-time in Santa Fe, and he hadn't been interested in listening to Andy fuss about him being gone all the time.

"Oh, well, I have a client." Andy wiggled his fingers at an older gent who sat at the bar. "You look amazing. All tanned and healthy."

"Thanks." He'd been helping Stoney while they hunted a maintenance man. He found he liked working alongside Stoney as an equal partner. "You look stellar as always."

"You're too kind and absolutely right." Little fuck. He did make Ford laugh. "Anyway, if you stay a few days, call me. We'll have lunch."

"Will do. Bye, Andy."

"See you, lovely!"

"So, was he like…?" Matt trailed off.

"We were. Five years ago or so." Ford winked. Andy was like Stoney's polar opposite, and Ford thought that was why he'd gone out with the guy. Slept with him. Never really lived with him.

Never loved him.

Ford couldn't say that about Stoney.

"He's kinda fussy, Ford." Matt clapped him on the back, damned near knocking him over. "Damn, it's good to get out of the house."

"You're a spoiled brat, man. You'll have to come up and see the ranch."

"I'd love that! Can I bring the kids?"

"God, yes. We have tons of shit for them to do." And if they didn't now, they would by the time Matt came up.

At least he hoped so.

Stoney would invent something. The man was magical with Quartz.

Matt handed him his wine and clinked their glasses together. "The twins still finish each other's sentences."

"Uh-huh." It was still weirdly hot. He grinned, the scent of garlic and tomato making him think of Geoff's pizza. What a homebody he was becoming.

Still, Stoney's gray eyes and warm smile and tight little butt were waiting at the ranch. Maybe he couldn't touch, but he could look. Dream.

Chapter Sixteen

JESUS Christ, look at the snow.

Ford had every available guy digging out Christmas lights, Geoff was testing out ten thousand things for Thanksgiving, Quartz was building a Ferris wheel or possibly the White House out of blocks, and him?

Stoney was sneaking a cigarette with Angie and Hetty in the tack room.

Stoney watched the snow falling as he took a drag. "Ty won't make it for Thanksgiving in this shit."

"Leastways you don't have guests to worry on, hmm?"

"That's right." Of course, no guests meant no money, but they had enough feed put in to last a bit. Ford had some diabolical plan for a party between now and Christmas, and Stoney was just nodding and smiling.

How were people supposed to get out here? Dogsleds?

That would be adorable. All those fancy-assed biggie wows that Ford lunched and dinner-dated with on sleds covered with dog fur and slobber. He'd pay to see that shit.

"What are you grinning about, monkey?" Angie asked.

"Oh, I'm just being an ass. Ford intends to have a big fancy-assed Christmas party up here."

"You need to grade the road, first." Hetty shook her head.

"Tell me how with all this snow and I'll be happy to." Stoney just wanted to go somewhere warm for a few days. Surely it was nice in Corpus.

"Oh, don't start. We're in for a hard winter, and we all know it. Ford will head out of here, and you won't see him till April, you watch and see." Angie sounded so sure, but he didn't know about that.

The man seemed perfectly happy to sit at his computer and work from the office at Ty's house.

His house. Whatever. Stoney wasn't sure he'd ever get used to Ty being gone, and God help them all if the snow kept Ty away. Quartz would lose his shit.

"So, fess up." Hetty kicked his ankle with the toe of her boot. "What the fuck is up with you and the metrosexual?"

"Up?"

"You know. What's the story? The whole story."

Stoney snorted. "It's a short story."

Hetty kicked him again, and Stoney sighed. "We were a thing in college. I went for a semester and a half. UNM. It was a fucking disaster, you know? I sucked at it, and Ford? Shit, he didn't. We came here on spring break, and I did some cowboy work for Ty and got myself a job. I went back and packed my shit and came to work. Ford was pissed."

"So you broke up with him?" Angie asked. "Did you tell him why?"

"I told him I got a job up here. I didn't tell him about failing out." That had been too much to bear, to admit he just wasn't good enough to do it.

"Oh man, no wonder he was pissy." Hetty grinned hugely. "You know how emotional gay guys get."

"Uh-huh. Because you giant dykes all wear white panties and ugly shoes while you grunt lullabies to your kids."

He could give as good as he got.

"My panties are plaid," Angie deadpanned.

"So why the fistfight in the yard?" Hetty was relentless once she smelled answers on the wind.

"I hit him in the office, not the yard."

"She's talking about when he tackled your skinny ass, not when you decked him and gave him his pretty bruise." Angie was a bitch; he adored her.

"Oh. We were talking about some family shit. Stuff he didn't know. He got a little grumpy when I walked out on the chat." The rest was no one else's business.

"Did it help?"

"We worked some shit out. It all settled." That part was actually true. Whatever butthurt Ford had about him and Brit, the man was being damn good to Quartz. In fact, he'd brought Quartz one of those how-it-was-built books from Aspen and turned the kid on to all of the miracle builder shows on Apple TV.

"Good deal. Y'all were kids. Obviously he's moved on and so have you."

Stoney nodded. "Obviously."

Ford had become this classy gay dude, and Stoney'd become a single dad in a world where gay cowboys were for rodeos and movies, mostly.

Angie gave him a shrewd look. "Of course, he's still single."

"We assume." No one knew anything about his life away from the ranch. Not a thing. Even Geoff only knew that Ford loved pizza—which Stoney remembered—and that he did tribal law for the most part. Water rights and shit.

Geoff could find out anything about anyone.

"Hmm. So have Geoff pump him for info." Hetty looked so proud of the idea.

"Right. I'm supposed to go to Geoff and say, 'Hey, man. Can you find out if Ford's fucking anybody right now? Seriously or otherwise. I just want to know where he's dipping his wick.'" Because that wouldn't be embarrassing. He didn't need to know. He had a healthy fantasy life involving Ford, thank you.

That had to be better than the reality, which would be getting turned down.

"I can totally do that," Geoff said, slipping into the barn. "I need to toke. Anyone want some?"

"Oh, for fuck's sake."

"What? We're all off the clock. It's five thirty, and the ladies aren't driving, right?"

"Nope. I did the feeding already." Hetty grinned at Stoney. "Your guest room open?"

"Always. Y'all know that."

"Rock on. Light 'er up, Geoffy. The boss needs a little unwinding."

Geoff pulled out the biggest doobie known to man and lit up, the acrid smell of green filling the space. Okay, so yeah, he would share.

"So, we're setting the boss up with Ford? That sort of rocks." Geoff blew out a stream of smoke. "Want a shotgun, boss?"

"You're a shit, and I adore you." He leaned forward, and Geoff took a long drag and held it a second before bringing their mouths together, feeding it to him.

Woo. There was something about a shotgun that made things much more intense.

"That is weirdly hot," Hetty said.

"You perv." Angie chuckled and kicked Geoff. "Share, man."

"You got it." Geoff passed it over with a grin.

Stoney felt the green start to relax him, his shoulders coming down from around his ears. Oh, man, that was good.

"You're all stressed out, boss." Geoff grabbed one of his hands and started massaging it.

"If we're sharing a joint, I'm not the boss."

"Sure you are. You also happen to be my friend." Geoff chuckled. "I hope everyone is okay with pizza and salad for supper. Quartz and Ford conspired."

"Sounds great. Tell me I get olives on mine." Geoff hit a tender spot, and Stoney moaned. "Oh, damn. That's sore."

"You got bruises popping up all on your knuckles."

Hetty cackled. "Punching Ford again?"

"Nah. Stable door caught me."

Both ladies winced. They knew how that went. Geoff hummed in sympathy and rubbed in long, gentle strokes, easing all his ouch.

Stoney drifted, wondering what Ford was doing, if he was alone at his desk. Maybe all the wheeling and dealing Ford did made him solitary when he had the chance, but what if he was lonely?

What if he was on his computer with a lover in Santa Fe? If there was one in Aspen, Ford could just run down, but not New Mexico. That was a ten-hour haul, at least.

"Definitely olives," Geoff said, snapping him back to the conversation. "I made a new dressing too."

"Stop with the food talk unless you brought a bag of Doritos," Hetty complained. "I'm hungry."

"Oh, Doritos…," they all spoke in concert.

"Will M&M's work?" Ford stepped in, shaking a bag of candy. "You guys totally suck."

"You want a hit? Totally legal, you know." Geoff grinned over at Ford as Angie and Hetty looked more like they were fixin' to die.

"Hell, yes. I only share if you do." Ford came over and sat on a hay bale.

"That's totally fair." Stoney refused to act all freaked. He tried to snatch the doobie from Angie's fingers so he could offer it over, but Geoff got hold of it first.

"You're not going to offer him a shotgun, boss?"

He was going to kill Geoff. Especially when Ford lit up like Christmas.

"Makes me cough less that way," Ford pointed out, and butter wouldn't melt in Ford's mouth.

"Well, I sure as shit won't let anyone else do it." Wait. Did he say that out loud?

Geoff chortled, handing over the joint, and yeah, he was going to do this. Ford leaned close, eyes closing, lashes dark on his cheeks.

Stoney took a deep hit and leaned forward. As he did, he heard Ford pass the bag of candy off to someone.

Then their lips met.

Shit. Stoney knew he was so fucked. He blew the smoke into Ford's mouth, a long stream of it, not wanting to let go.

Ford slid his hand up Stoney's arm, holding them together for just another second.

His lungs burned, and Stoney had to pull back, blinking to try to right the world once more.

"That was… something." Ford breathed deep.

"Uh-huh." He stared until Ford opened his eyes, a weird little smile on his face.

Ford glanced around. "Uh. I didn't mean to scare off everyone."

Sure enough, the only things still with them were the joint and the M&M's.

"Oh… I…. They didn't take the green."

"Yeah." Ford plucked the doobie from him to take a drag, then grabbed Stoney behind the head with the other hand to draw him close and return the favor.

His eyes rolled back in his head, his cock as hard as nails as the smoke passed between them. He clenched his hands into fists to keep from ripping Ford's clothes right off. They were in the barn. In November. Smoking weed.

Ford never stopped touching, the fingertips brushing the short hairs on the back of Stoney's head the most erotic thing he'd ever felt.

When they finally sat back, they simply looked at each other. Both of them breathing hard.

"I want you, Stoney." Just like that. As if knowing the truth had turned off Ford's anger.

"Yeah." He got that. He was going to disappoint them both, though. Stoney knew it before Ford reached for him again. "No."

Ford's lips thinned. "No?"

"Not like this, man. I want you more than I want to breathe, but I don't want neither of us to say we didn't know what we were doing. I want to remember every second."

Ford sat back, his frown fading. "No shit. Okay. I can see that. Agree even."

"Yeah." He reached out, touched Ford's bottom lip, dragged his finger over the sweet flesh, which was a little swollen already.

"I—you. Okay, I want pizza if we're not gonna be all over each other." Ford grinned at him, so much like the man he fell in love with for a moment that Stoney's heart clenched in his chest.

"Get on, then. I'm gonna wait for this"—he waved at his crotch—"to go down."

Ford snorted. "Just do what I do. Use a handful of snow."

"I always knew you were a sick son of a bitch." Stoney had to grin, though. Had to.

"Hell, yes. Use what nature gives you. That's what I always say." Ford swooped in to give him a kiss that made his ears ring. "Soon, Stoney. I know how good it could be now."

"Soon. We got things to say to each other." Naked things.

Ford nodded, then turned on his heel and left. Stoney had to admit, he felt odd, being the one who watched Ford walk off. He usually stomped out of their encounters.

He stubbed out the joint and stashed it, then grabbed a handful of M&M's. Lord help him, he was a stupid motherfucker.

Stupid, but fixin' to get laid soon.

Chapter Seventeen

THE crunch of tires on gravel and ice surprised Ford. He heard it from the bathroom, where he'd just turned on the shower. Helping with the feeding had left him frozen near to death. Damn it. Couldn't be Ty. He wouldn't be in for another two days….

Ah, screw it. Stoney was in the kitchen. He could handle whoever it was for a few minutes, right?

If it was a guest, they'd be coming to the office anyway. He was fairly sure even the one family they had booked was going to cancel with the current forecast.

Ford stepped into the steamy shower, glad he'd gone ahead and put in another water heater. He was upgrading all sorts of mechanical and system type stuff a little at a time. There wasn't all that much. Hell, Stoney was a methodical man who kept things running.

He just needed help with the bigger picture. Ford was super strong at the overview, at making things new.

They hadn't managed to hook up yet. Quartz had been stuck in the house and needing attention, and Ford had a couple of deals that had gone to hell. However, every time their eyes met, that spark flared to life again.

Hope was a relatively new emotion for Ford. He tended to think it was cruel. Stoney gave him hope, though, now that Ford knew the full story of the past. Hell, it felt a lot like Stoney had been waiting for him all these years.

His finger traced the same pattern Stoney's had that night in the barn, his body tightening at the memory. God, he wanted that body, that smile. He wanted to see if Stoney was braver now, or if he'd still be oddly shy.

Now was not the time, though. Not even for a happy fantasy jack off. Who knew who was out there?

He had to admit that he was a little worried about leaving a certain Texan cowboy out there to deal with some hotshot from Aspen. If one of his business contacts showed up and Stoney said the wrong thing.... It wasn't a trust issue. This was more that Stoney wasn't a people person.

He dried off, then dragged on a pair of jeans and a turtleneck, a heavy pair of socks and his boots. The heat was something Stoney wanted to work on naturally, supplementing with woodstoves and some solar, but in the meantime, Ford was freezing his ass off. His adobe walls in Santa Fe held in the heat so much better.

Maybe he'd go home for a few days, soon. Enjoy the farolitos, the hot chocolate, the pinyon smoke on the air.

Right on the heels of that thought, though, was that if he did go, he would need to take Stoney and Quartz at least, and maybe Geoff. Then where would that leave his open house in mid-December?

Maybe he'd go in January, after all.

Ford combed his hair, which was getting a bit long, and splashed on some smell good. He chuckled, because he'd stopped doing that when he went to college. Once a rancher, always one, right?

He heard soft laughter as he moved toward the kitchen. "…no ma'am. It's not usually quite so busy in here, but with the holidays, Geoff, our head chef, is on fire."

Ford paused, peering around the doorjamb into the kitchen, trying to stay out of sight.

"And you have a dining room?" the slight lady with the teased hair asked.

"We have a family dining room, yes, but we're planning a big old space for parties, for get-togethers. I imagine it'll open up this summer, just in time for weddings."

Was that his Stoney? Ford watched him charm the lady who'd dropped in, smiling and giving her the ten-cent tour.

"Would you like to see the main guest cabin?" Stoney asked. "Ford, that's Tyson's nephew, has done it up Santa Fe style in the last month. We've also gone really energy efficient. I see you got your good snow boots on."

"I'd love to, Mr. River."

"Oh, ma'am, call me Stoney. Please. We've had our handshakes and howdies. Let me see if Miss Miranda is available to walk with us. She's a sweetheart and the lady you'll speak with on the phone should you call. She loves to put a face with a name."

Oh good man. Stoney managed to get Miranda to come with them so no one would feel uncomfortable while making it clear that wasn't why he was doing it at all. Classy.

Stoney headed toward the back door, pulling on his coat. "Maybe Geoff will be back when we swing by and we can try a pastry."

Ford bit back a chuckle. Stoney had said that loud enough for Ford to hear, so he needed to rustle up Geoff and get some coffee going.

He texted Stoney with "*on it*" and then texted Geoff.

"*On my way*," Geoff texted back, so Ford tackled the espresso machine.

Geoff came running, man bun flopping. "Dude. No. You are totally not cleared to touch. Not notty not not. Hands off my baby."

"But you need to produce buns. Croissants. Something." He'd been a barista once, in grad school.

"I have cherry danish or cinnamon buns I can heat up. Who is she?"

"No idea. My guess is local reporter or Chamber of Commerce for Carbondale or Glenwood. Too old-school and Western for Aspen."

She reminded Ford of his gran, in fact.

"Ah. Then cinnamon buns. Cherry can get messy."

"I like that you have a stock."

Geoff herded Ford to a stool. "Hunters. You never know when they'll get frustrated and want to come back to civilization. I prefer fresh, but I always have something to defrost."

Ford shook his head. "I can help."

"This is what I live for."

"Okay, but I'm here for you, man." Ford grinned. Sooner or later, someone would want him to assist.

"Grab some plates for me?"

"You got it." Geoff had amassed a ridiculous array of weird china plates, apparently from yard saling with Angie. He pulled out several, checking for chips.

"There are some doilies too, but I'm always afraid that reads old queen to people."

Jesus, Geoff was a dork.

"I think we'll settle for the good plates. Maybe a cake plate for your creations. I might qualify as old, but not you."

"Shit. You're what? Thirty-three like the boss? We might not have been in high school together, but it's close."

"Uh-huh. You're still young enough for optimism and all that shit." Ford grabbed pretty coffee mugs. Teacups seemed too dainty.

"Yeah, but I saw you in the barn. You have hope."

The sadness in Geoff's voice would have surprised him except that Stoney's story was still fresh in his brain. Found beaten half to death for daring to be caught gay.

Ford surprised himself, and Geoff, by giving the guy a spontaneous hug. "Don't give up, buddy."

"I'm cool. My body's a temple, you know?"

Right. A temple. Fuck that shit.

Ford blinked at himself. Now that wasn't a very understanding thought. That sounded like Stoney. When you lived like a cowboy, he guessed.

"Temples get worshipped," Ford quipped. "Now, coffee."

"Macchiato? Latte? Americano?"

"Let me text Stoney."

It took no time for the answer of "caramel lattes if cherry. If cinnamon, Mexican mocha."

Okay, this was moving from impressive into absolutely adorable. These two clearly had a guest routine, and it was totally working for Ford. He just needed to capitalize on it.

Geoff made coffees, and Ford watched, wheels turning in his brain.

Voices sounded, and then the trio appeared, both women laughing, Stoney taking coats. "Oh, y'all. Here are the other two hooligans I was telling Miss Val about. This is Geoff, the best chef on the Western Slope, and this is the new co-owner of the ranch, Ford Nixel. Y'all, this here's Miss Val from *The Sentinel* over in Grand Junction, just to chat with us."

"Well, good morning, Miss Val," Geoff said, a heart-melting smile on his face. "I hope you like cinnamon rolls."

"Oh, I adore them. I swear, you are the most accommodating place. There are good bones here, stunning views."

"Stoney's done a great job maintaining the integrity of the ranch," Ford said, holding out a hand. "We're working on the next level now."

She took his hand, obviously at ease and primed for his sale of the new things he had planned. Ford was frickin' impressed. Stoney knew his shit.

Ford smiled. "Have a seat. You have to try Geoff's rolls and coffee."

By the time the food was oohed and aahed over and the lattes—complete with hearts in the crema, thank you very much—were devoured, Miranda had an Easter egg hunt booked, a glowing article assured, and the name of a contact for advertising in the paper.

Stoney quietly did dishes and refilled coffees while Ford talked solar energy and cisterns, and Geoff promised to share his icing recipe with the food editor.

All in all, Ford thought it went really well.

"Mr. Stoney," Val said as the cowboy was helping her with her coat. "It was a pleasure to meet you."

"Oh, I'm so glad you drove up. Next time I'm down in the Junction to visit, we should have lunch together. You can show me around some."

She blushed and fluttered, the gentle flirting just perfect. "Well, you have my card. Mr. Nixel, I hope I'll get an invite to the open house."

"Yes, ma'am," Ford agreed. "I'll send those invites out just after Thanksgiving."

"Perfect. Happy Thanksgiving."

"I'll walk you to your car. There's a touch of ice."

"So kind." Miss Val took Stoney's arm, and they walked out.

Ford shook his head. "Stoney's really good at that."

They didn't even pretend to not know what he was talking about.

Miranda nodded, her wild red hair flying everywhere. "That man loves people, and it shows. You hear cowboy and you think 'alone on the prairie,' but Stoney gets guests in here and he comes to life."

"We have a lot of repeat families, thanks to him," Geoff agreed. "He's just not an innovator."

"He's fine like he is." Magical, even. Ford could feel ideas building in his brain like rainbow-colored bubbles.

"Geoff?" Quartz came in, holding a broken plate in his hands, eyes down. "I dropped this on the floor. I'm sorry."

"Hey, buddy. That's okay. You know why?" Geoff took the pieces, carefully examining Quartz's hands in the process.

"'Cause you're not mad?"

"No, because you told me instead of hiding it. Stuff breaks, but you have to be honest about it. I'm proud of you."

"Yes, sir. Can I have the broom? There's some sharp bits."

"You bet. Be super careful, okay?" Geoff handed over the broom.

Mira popped the last bite of pastry into her mouth. "Gotta get back to the office. Payroll to run."

"Everybody wants their preholiday checks," Geoff said. "You staying for Thanksgiving?"

"Nope. Boyfriend is meeting the parents."

"Neat! Have fun."

Ford winked at Geoff. "I'll be here. I expect all the trimmings." He knew Geoff had been experimenting for days. Weeks.

"You, me, Angie and Hetty, both the wranglers, Quartz and Stoney, and I think the Hollisters are coming too. She's got a brand-new baby, and Stoney told them to bring the kids and let us cook."

"I don't think Ty will make it," Ford said, keeping his voice low. "Sophia is iffy anyway, and the weather is bad."

"He'll come before Christmas, and we'll have a thing, huh?"

"Oh, that ought to make Quartz happy, right?"

"What should?" Stoney asked, slipping back into the room and rubbing his hands to warm them.

"Ty coming out before Christmas, but after Thanksgiving."

"As long as Quartz gets to see him, we'll be cool. I already explained about the weather, and he's tickled his Uncle Ford is here." Stoney winked at Ford as if to say he didn't get that at all.

"Yeah, yeah." Quartz was different from other kids Ford knew, not that he knew many. Most of his buddies in Santa Gay were double income, no kids types.

He had to wonder what they'd say, if they saw him now.

They would probably tease him unmercifully, but he really found he didn't care. Not with Stoney grinning at him like that.

"Daddy? Are you busy? Can you come listen to me read?"

Stoney nodded. "I can. Then you can come help me feed."

"Uncle Ford helped!"

"Not with the cows out in the high pasture." Stoney rolled his eyes. "Little shit."

"That's deep snow out there, huh?"

"Yeah, we'll whistle them down. They'll come."

Ford nodded. "Holler if you need help. I could play a cowboy on TV, at least."

"Will do." Stoney patted him on the arm, the act just as natural as breathing. They'd touched a lot more in the last few days than they had when they were together, even. Both older, maybe, more comfortable in their skin.

Maybe they were both just home.

The thought made Ford stop, blink. Home.

He'd thought that was a condo in Aspen or an adobe off Canyon Road in Santa Fe.

Ford was beginning to think it was more than that.

Chapter Eighteen

THE blizzard set in the night before Thanksgiving.

The snow began falling again around three in the afternoon, and by five, one thing became totally clear to Stoney. They needed to get all the horses in, no matter where they were pastured, and the small herd of cattle they ran needed to be moved to the closest pasture where he could monitor the stock tanks, and feed most easily with the supplemental feed.

He got his heaviest socks and his longies on and grabbed his heavy flannel to go under his long coat. This was a hell of a lot easier in Texas, he swore to God.

"Daddy, where are you going?"

"We got to move the horses, son. You hang here."

"I can help."

Stoney tried not to scowl. "Yep, you can. Get all the dogs who don't herd inside, and get with Geoff to make coffee and snacks. We'll all need it when we get back."

Angie and Doc could four-wheel, but him and Tanner would have to ride. They'd put the packhorses out a ways after the last hunting party to give them the best grazing and rest. Now he'd kick his own ass for that if he could reach it.

"But, Daddy…."

"What did I say?" He didn't have time for this shit.

"Yessir." Quartz's shoulders slumped, and Stoney pondered checking in with Ford to make sure he kept an eye on Quartz. Geoff would be in the kitchen in less than a minute….

"Come on, boss! We got to get this done before the storm gets worse."

"I'm fully aware of that." He fastened a look on Quartz. "You wait here for Geoff, okay? Stay out of trouble, you hear?"

"Yes, Daddy."

Quartz's lower lip pooched out, but he wouldn't disobey a direct order like that, so Stoney turned on his heel, barking orders at Tanner. He headed out into the storm, the breath whooshing out of him for a moment.

Geoff passed them on the way in. "You got your radio?"

"Uh-huh. Y'all have warm stuff waiting." Stoney headed out to the barn, the wind already screaming. He wrapped his scarf around his face even tighter as the wind tried to steal it. He'd need that wool mother to breathe into, keep his nose from freezing.

He pulled himself up on Button, saluting Tanner in thanks for saddling her up. He would cut up the most direct path to the packhorses, while Tanner would swing around on his surefooted gelding to come at them from the top.

Angie waved when she drove off, and he said a little prayer for every one of his hands, dogs, and livestock. Prayer was never in vain, right?

Right. God loved dogs, horses, and stupid fucking cowboys.

Chapter Nineteen

FORD stared out the window, worry riding him like a drunk cowboy riding a calf backward—9:00 p.m. and Stoney and their drover, Tanner, still weren't back. Angie and Doc had been back by seven, but they'd been on four-wheelers....

The wind howled, and Ford glanced at Geoff, who sat nearby, playing cribbage with Quartz. "Try the radio again?"

"They're out of range, man. That's all. With this weather, it's no surprise. They had to check the mustangs too." Still, Geoff did it, didn't he? Because they were all there in the kitchen, worrying.

Angie waited until Geoff got nothing but static before snapping her book back together. "I'm going after them."

"No." Ford bit the word out like a bullet. "We need you here. They both have avalanche beacons. If they were in real trouble, they would trigger those."

"But—"

He fastened her with a look. *Not in front of Quartz, dammit. Don't scare the boy.*

Angie nodded, lips tight. She managed a smile for Quartz then. "Right. Hopefully they get back in range soon."

"I would go with you, Miss Angela. Doogie says I'm a good cowboy. He says it's in my blood." Quartz had this expression on his face that Ford remembered from Brit. Stubborn, determined, and utterly fearless. It had gotten her killed; he'd be damned if he let that same urge kill her boy.

"No one else is going out there before morning." The thought tore at his gut. Hell, if Stoney made it home, Ford would thaw him out, then tear his ass up. No more waiting. "Can you imagine what would happen if you went out there and got lost, Quartz? Your daddy has enough to worry about."

"Your Uncle Ford is right, honey." Angie sighed softly. "We got no way to know where he is, and you can't see nothin' with the snow."

The door opened, and they all looked up, then sighed as it was Hetty coming in from checking the horses. "There's a half dozen not in, but those packhorses are tough. Heard from Tanner and Stoney yet?"

Angie shook her head.

"Damn." Hetty stomped to the stove, where Geoff had left the oven door open a crack between bakes. Apparently, Geoff baked when he was stressed.

Good thing Thanksgiving was tomorrow, huh?

Ford chewed on his bottom lip, trying not to stare out the window at the blizzard raging just beyond the glass. Stoney was out there. Damn.

"Be right back," Quartz said when he and Geoff finished a game. "Bathroom."

Ford nodded, half his attention on the radio, which stayed silent.

He caught the barest glimpse of someone with a bright red hat heading for the barns about five minutes later. A shorter than your average cowboy someone.

Oh, he didn't think so.

"Geoff, get some hot chocolate on, stat." Ford grabbed his coat and hustled out the door, going to catch Quartz before he did something super stupid.

The last thing they needed was Quartz freezing to death alongside his father. Explaining that to Uncle Ty would cause him stress.

He caught Quartz just before he pulled a big gelding out of a stall, a lead clipped to his harness. "I'm pretty sure this is not staying put, kiddo."

"I…. I…. That's my daddy. I can't just let him… be lost. That's my daddy!"

"He's not lost." Ford put every bit of certainty he had into the words. "Who knows this ranch better than anyone but your grandpa?"

"My daddy. My daddy rides every inch of this land, but…." Quartz looked outside where there was nothing but white.

Yeah.

Yeah, Ford knew.

"Do you and your daddy pray together, kiddo?" He knew Stoney had grown up fairly religious; he just had no idea if he was passing that on to Quartz.

"Yes, sir. Every night. Daddy says that praying helps God help us be our best selves."

"Well, He also helps us when we need it. Maybe we could go back and have Angie and Geoff say a little prayer with us."

It was too cold for this shit.

"You promise that he'll come home, that he won't think I was bad for not rescuing him?"

"What did he tell you to do?" Ford asked, knowing Stoney had told Quartz no playing cowboy.

"Stay here and make sure Geoff had hot stuff ready for him when he came home."

"Your daddy is a cowboy and so is Tanner. They will be back."

"Okay." Quartz's voice got very small, and he grabbed Ford's hand. "I'm scared."

"Which is when we have to be our bravest. That was why you were willing to ride out. Come on, kiddo. Back to the house." Quartz unclipped the lead, and Ford made sure the big gelding was secure in his stall.

"Should I give everyone a scoop of sweet feed, Uncle?"

"I think you should. That's a great idea. Extra warmth, right?" While Quartz did that, Ford did a quick check to make sure none of the horses needed a blanket or had hoof issues.

By the time they made it back, Hetty and Angie were heading out to find them, both women scowling.

Ford smiled easily. "Just checking the horses. I gave old Smokey a blanket."

Hetty caught the look on his face and smiled back. "Cool beans. Those packhorses will want a warm place to land as soon as they get back."

"I got feed ready," Quartz said. "And the floor heat is on."

"Good man. Come on inside with me and show me how to play this card game." Hetty held out a hand to Quartz and took him inside.

Angie hung back to stare hard at Ford. "Nice save."

"Thanks. How much longer do we realistically give him before we call someone?"

Angie snorted. "You're right. No one should leave before first light."

"I hate being right." Ford chuckled. "I really do."

"Me too. I should have ridden with them."

"And what? They'll be home. The storm's just slowing them down." Ford was going to maintain a positive fucking attitude, right? "I ran off after Ty once when I was fourteen. Got lost. I didn't sit down for a week."

"Oh, damn." She winced, shook her head, as they stamped their boots clean. "Did you live with him? I mean, what about your folks?"

"My dad died when I was five. Car accident." Ford shrugged. "Mom lost her shit and left. Gran was around too, but she passed from lung cancer when I was in college."

"That sucks, man. Truly. Ty's a good man, though."

"He is." Ford could totally understand that Ty would do whatever he had to in order to preserve the ranch for Quartz. That was what the old man had done for Ford, after all. Ty had done it for Brit too. He had to wonder, though, what would have happened to Stoney if Brit hadn't died.

He tilted his head. Okay, stupid as it was, it had just hit him that Ty had done all this for Stoney too. So the man always had a home. He wasn't sure if he was proud of Ty or a little aggravated because Stoney wasn't fucking stupid.

"You gonna stand there and freeze solid?" Angie asked him.

"Not when Geoff is baking."

"Excellent point. Come on. There's food and coffee."

They made their way inside, stopping in the mudroom to stomp their boots clean. Quartz burst in on them, wreathed in smiles.

"Tanner radioed! They're coming. They found a horse down. He wasn't ours, but it took them an hour to get him up and looped to Tanner's gelding."

"Thank God."

Quartz nodded. "Yes. Thank you, God! You did good!"

Angie laughed out loud. "Geoff! I need some special creamer in my coffee!"

"Not until we get those horses in and wrap the boss and Tanner in warm blankets." Geoff grinned at Quartz. "Go get a bunch of towels and toss them in the dryer, little man."

"Okay!" Quartz tore off, and Ford chuckled.

"What should I do, boss?" he asked Geoff.

"Tanner said they'd be about a half hour out, so I guess we wait."

"I'll get a couple of lights set up then." Ford couldn't just sit on his hands.

"Works for me. Stoney and Tanner are coming home." Geoff looked about as happy as a clam.

"It's about damned time. I'll take some special creamer too, once the work is done."

"Yessir. Baileys for all."

"Good man."

Hetty returned once Geoff went back to the kitchen. "Help you with those lights."

"Yes, ma'am. I'd appreciate it." Hell, he was flying. He hadn't realized how much he'd been holding his breath until he'd heard Stoney was coming back. Safe and sound.

Thank God. Now he just had to stay busy until Stoney walked through the door.

Chapter Twenty

STONEY was cold down into the marrow of his bones, he swore. Him and Tanner hadn't spoken a word in the last forty-five minutes—there just wasn't the energy, and they had to get these horses home.

He checked the compass and kept them heading south, knowing the ranch had to be there. Had to be where he left it.

The trip down was even more grueling because they were herding, and because they had a half-starved horse looped between them, two ropes keeping the beast on its feet.

The light from the barns was the most welcome sight in history, a beacon shining from the snow.

"Red carpet's out," Tanner croaked, and Stoney chuckled.

"Yessir. Hot showers and coffee and a soft bed." He hadn't let himself be scared, not until he saw the house, then he started to shake in his gloves.

His teeth chattered, and he almost slid out of the saddle, but they had at least a quarter mile to go and horses to settle, at least one to doctor.

A little boy to hug.

Quartz had to be losing his mind. That kept Stoney going all the way down to the barn, where Angie and Hetty and Doc all waited for them.

"Y'all get in the house. We got this." Angie clapped him on the shoulder. "Boss."

He didn't have any words, so he grabbed Tanner and pushed them across the huge expanse of yard and into the kitchen.

Geoff and Ford met them with hot towels and even hotter coffee, as well as tons of soft clothes. "Showers in a few, but we can't warm you up too fast. Your heart could stop," Ford said.

"Daddy! Daddy!" Quartz tackled him, and he went down. His feet felt like blocks of wood, and he couldn't keep on them.

"I'm right here." Stoney gasped for breath while Quartz clung to him.

"Daddy! You're cold! Uncle Ford, we have to help?"

"Shh. Shh. I'm…." Christ, he couldn't stop shaking.

"Come on, Stoney. Geoff has Tanner." Ford hauled his ass up off the floor and took him back to his bedroom, Quartz trailing too. "Quartz, get the covers back and get the warm towels in the bed. Let's get these clothes off you."

"I…." Shouldn't he be helping? He blinked at Ford, just feeling a little like he was stuck in a loop.

"You're frozen, huh? Just hold on."

Stoney felt as if his skin was going to shatter like glass by the time Ford stuffed him under the covers.

Ford climbed in on top of the sheets, pushing close, and Quartz came in on the other side. The immediate warmth shocked him, his body jerking.

"Shh." Ford pulled the blankets up around his neck tight. "In and out, Stoney. Breathe with me. Try to relax your muscles."

"Sorry." His teeth couldn't stop chattering, and he latched on to Ford's gaze, the dark eyes damn near hypnotic.

"We got this, right? Quartz, get us some more towels, huh?"

"Uh-huh. Hot ones, Uncle?"

When had Quartz become close enough to Ford to sound so easy?

"Please. Make sure Tanner is okay too, okay?"

"Uh-huh. Be right back." Quartz sounded like a herd of rampaging elephants on his way down the hall.

Ford caught Stoney's gaze again. "Come on now, baby. You have to breathe." Ford leaned in until they were sharing air, which helped Stoney stop hiccuping.

Cold out there. That was what he'd meant to say, at any rate. What came out was more, "Co… Co… Co…." But it was close.

"You were out too long. Damn it, Stoney." Ford kissed him. Full on the mouth. Hard.

If he was dead in a ditch somewhere, this was the best Heaven ever.

Ever.

Ford pressed him down into the covers, and everything started to sparkle a little. He moaned, the sound making room for a little more heat. All he could do was let Ford warm him up, love on him.

"I have you. Going to beat you, scaring me so much."

He lay there, just blinking at Ford's words.

"You scared Quartz half to death too." Ford chuckled as the thunder came back down the hall.

"Uh-huh. He's… coming. You… kissed me."

"I did. I decided no more waiting. I mean, I'll thaw you out and let you sleep, but then I am going after your ass."

"Promises, promises…."

"Daddy! Towels, and Geoff warmed up blankets and hot water bottles."

"Good deal." Ford rose up and grabbed Quartz, dragging him right into the pile again. "How's Tanner?"

"Kinda blue. Geoff is going to put him in the shower once his fingers and toes start moving." Quartz leaned in. "You scared me, Daddy. Did you get all the horses?"

"All plus one."

"Really? Was he really cold?"

"He was. He was stuck in a ravine. Tanner and I couldn't leave him there."

"Can I help nurse him?" Quartz asked.

"You have to ask Hetty."

"Listen to that, Quartz. His teeth have almost stopped chattering," Ford murmured.

"'Cause he's telling me no."

"Did not, butthead child."

Quartz's lip quivered. "I love you, Daddy. Is it okay if I have a cookie before I get ready for bed?"

"I love you." He grabbed his son, held on with hands that were screaming with nerves. "Thank you, son, for being good."

"I tried, Daddy." Quartz gave Ford an odd glance before scampering off, still clearly freaked out.

"He okay? I need to…." Stoney felt fuzzy as all get-out.

"You need to rest. I'm going to get you something hot to drink. You stay here, and I'll check on Quartz." Ford kissed him again, which really made him wonder if he'd frozen to death.

He dozed off and on, then after it seemed like just seconds, Ford was back, shaking him. "Come on, baby. Water."

"You haven't called me that since junior year," Stoney said.

"I haven't called you. Come on, drink up. Water, then some hot tea."

"Coffee?" Hot tea was for sick people, right?

Ford snorted. "Tomorrow morning, absolutely."

"But—"

"You need rest, not caffeine. Quartz had a cookie, and Angie is putting him to bed with a list of chores he has for the new horse." Ford held a water bottle to Stoney's lips.

He drank deep, his eyelids feeling so like it took effort to blink them. "I wasn't going to get lost out there."

Stoney had reasons to be home. Some new, some forever.

"I know. I told Quartz you'd come back. We did freak out a bit when we couldn't get you on the radio." Ford's voice broke a little.

"There were some tough parts." When Tanner had misjudged the way down the mountain. That had scared the living fuck out of him. Tanner was a trooper, though, and had short roped that new mare all the way down to the ranch. "Is Tanner okay?"

"Geoff is getting him thawed. He needs better boots. Or he needs to stay on his horse more. Your feet look pretty good, but he was getting some early signs of frostbite."

"He had one hell of a fall. Me, not so much." He'd been lucky this time. Next time, who knew?

"We'll talk about some procedures. Later." Ford fed Stoney a few more sips of water, then some tea.

The tea was sweet, spicy, and hot, and it felt good going all the way down. Stoney closed his eyes and breathed deep, his ribs loosening finally.

"There you go." Ford kept touching him—his wrist, his collarbone, his ribs. Finally, Ford set the tea aside and stood, but didn't leave. Ford just stripped down in order to crawl into bed with him.

"Hey." Stoney was about 110 percent sure he couldn't get it up, but he wasn't going to kick Ford out for eating crackers.

"Shh. Just hush, okay? I need to hold you for a bit." Ford snuggled close, reminding him of that first time they'd slept together, Ford renting them a hotel room so they didn't have to share a single at the dorms. They'd always fit together like a dream, like they belonged, with his head on Ford's shoulder.

Stoney wrapped himself up in Ford and closed his eyes. He had a lot of thanks to give.

He swore he felt Ford's lips brush the top of his head as he drifted off to sleep.

Stoney sure hoped his brain wasn't froze. This was too good to be a dream.

Chapter Twenty-One

FORD woke up late, and he knew it because of the way the sun slanted across the floor. Hell, he never left his curtains open, so why was the sun creeping in anyway?

He opened his eyes, finding himself in Stoney's room, alone. There was a steaming cup of coffee and a blueberry muffin sitting there on the bedside table.

Well, there went that little fantasy of waking Stoney with some hot rubbing and bumping.

Time to get moving.

Still, someone had left the treat for him, hadn't they? Ford was gonna take that as a good sign. He crept from Stoney's room to his so he could grab a quick shower and get dressed.

He made it to the hallway when he ran into Stoney, the man still in his socks.

"Hey." Ford waved the muffin. "Thanks."

"You're welcome." He got a shy little smile, Stoney looking surprisingly young without his cowboy uniform.

"Still got all your toes?" Ford asked.

"It looks like. We got another foot of snow overnight. We'll all be hanging out for a few. I'm letting Hetty and Angie borrow the snowmobiles to check their horses after dinner."

"Good deal. Any word from Ty?" Ford was pretty sure he knew the answer, and honestly he would feel better if Ty stayed down in the Junction.

"I told him they had to stay there. No one needs to be driving in this shit."

"Good man. Quartz has a new horse to distract him, right?"

"God, yes. He's all *Black Stallion* about this one."

"Well, that means the poor thing will get good treatment, that's for sure." Ford chuckled. "No brand on it?"

"Nope. As bad shape as this thing was in, there's no way he's a stray."

"Poor thing." Ford shifted from foot to foot. "You, uh, get a shower already?"

"Just fixin' to grab one. Angie has Quartz in the barn."

"Wanna save water?" He wasn't going to pussyfoot around. They were both adults, and Ford wanted to see for himself that Stoney was all there and safe.

Stoney licked his lips, the move pure, unadulterated hunger. "I can handle that, yessir."

"I bet my bathroom is bigger." Also a lot less of a chance there of Quartz walking in on them.

Stoney gave him a short, sharp nod, touched his wrist. The tiny motions made Ford hard as nails, made his belly ache.

He sucked in a deep breath before grabbing Stoney's hand and slipping down the hall. God, he wanted to run, to shout.

More than that, he didn't want anyone to interrupt him. He needed some time to look and touch and kiss. Stroke.

God, he wanted to stroke Stoney off and make him shoot. He wanted to see and smell and taste. He tugged Stoney into the bathroom and began yanking off clothes.

"Doors are locked?" Stoney tore at his belt buckle.

"Yes." God help him, he was going to strain something getting his damned jeans back off, and he'd barely gotten them on.

"Good."

His cock pushed right out toward Stoney's fingers, like there wasn't anything else on earth his body wanted to do. Ford refused to let this be weird. He just let it happen, Stoney's fingers closing tightly on him.

"Oh, I remember this." Stoney looked at him as if he were breakfast.

"I'm not sure I do, so that's impressive." Ford hadn't exactly been celibate, but the last few years had been a hell of a dry spell.

"I couldn't forget you." Stoney turned bright red and pushed into his lips, kissing him stupid.

Ford moaned, wrapping his arms around Stoney's waist. He'd wanted this so badly since they'd had it out about Brit, since he knew that Stoney still needed him.

Since he'd gotten that shotgun, breathed in Stoney's air.

He grunted when he got Stoney out of those jeans, their skin meeting when it was finally bare. Oh, fuck, no one had ever felt this way. No one but Stoney made his heart race and his freaking knees weak.

Jesus, he was losing his goddamn mind.

"I want…." Stoney rocked against him, and Ford remembered he had hands. They could really give each other some happy touching.

"Shower. We should…." He grabbed hold of Stoney, though, stroked him from base to tip, over and over.

"Yes. Oh, there." Stoney showed him where there was by rubbing under the head of Ford's cock with the tip of his thumb.

His jaw clenched, electricity shooting through him, snapping from his balls to the base of his neck. Ford danced, hips rocking. He wasn't even going to make it into the water.

Hell, he wasn't even going to make it to turning on the water.

Ford flicked his thumb where Stoney had touched him, giving the feeling right back. Stoney's teeth sank into his own bottom lip, and Ford grinned, even though he was fairly sure he looked like he was just going to eat Stoney alive.

"More, Ford. Christ, it's been so long." Stoney didn't appear worried at all.

"Yeah. Tell me about it." Later. Stoney could tell him all about it after they both shot.

Stoney laughed, tugging at Ford's cock with both hands, making him grit his teeth, his belly pulling in tight. He matched Stoney, stroke for stroke, both of them right there, teetering on the edge.

Finally Ford knew he was about to go right over, so he leaned in to kiss Stoney hard, stealing their breath clean away.

He wouldn't know, after the fact, who shot first, but it didn't matter. They both grunted, heat splashing over hands, balls emptying.

Ford swayed, and Stoney caught him, the embrace natural, both of them holding on.

Their lips met, the kiss starting slow, but he could feel the fire building between them. He backed off and got the shower going, more than a little in love with the tankless water heater Stoney had apparently bullied Ty into a few years ago. The steam started almost immediately, and Ford tugged Stoney with a hand on one hip, getting them into the shower. Time was a luxury since it was Thanksgiving, and he wanted one more go at that lean, hard body.

Stoney took a deep breath when the hot water hit him and stepped right into the curve of Ford's body.

"You look amazing." There were scars now, and some lines that hadn't been there, but now Ford didn't have to imagine what a fully mature Stoney looked like naked. He knew.

"Do I look different to you?" Stoney's hand slipped down his belly, not heading for his cock, he didn't think, more just petting.

"Some. I mean, we're both a lot older, right?" Ford hoped he looked good to Stoney.

"You look better. Stronger. You're so fucking pretty." The praise sounded like prayer from Stoney's lips.

"I've dreamed about you, baby." That was the truth. Somewhere deep inside he'd never given up the idea that he would get Stoney back.

Stoney's deep gray gaze shot to his, burning up at him. "No shit?"

"Nope. I was so fucking mad," Ford said, then shook his head. No. None of that now. This was for touching. Loving. "Now I just want you."

"I'll piss you off again, eventually. Let's take what we can get."

Ford laughed, then nodded. "Probably. Kiss me, Stoney."

Stoney ran both hands back up his chest, fingers barely teasing his nipples before they wrapped around his shoulders, and Stoney went up on tiptoe, tongue ramming between his lips.

Ford moaned, sliding one arm around that strong back, pressing them together. His cock rose hard again, surprising him, and Stoney stepped even closer, totally unafraid to snuggle up to him.

They slipped and slid together, the hot water easing the way, the steam keeping them shrouded in a world of their own. At some point the soap came into play and the scent of sandalwood and citrus filled the air.

"Nice." Stoney rubbed a cloth over Ford's chest.

"Mmm. I buy it at the Loretto in Santa Fe. There's a soap shop." He raised his arms when Stoney scrubbed at his ribs, making him laugh.

"I like it." Stoney surprised him, nibbling at his nipple.

"Uhn." His toes curled up, his cock jerking.

He felt Stoney grin. Little shit. Then the bite came again, the sensation like a hit of fire.

"Teasing man." He tangled his fingers in the wet length of Stoney's hair. Ford held on, this whole situation like a fantasy come true.

"Just want to... can I?" Stoney knelt down, and Ford's heart stopped for a second.

Could he?

Fuck yes.

Words failed Ford, so he pushed forward with his hips, his cock rubbing along Stoney's cheekbone. The stubble rasped him, and the soft touch of Stoney's tongue made him feel weak-kneed.

He shook, fingers tracing the contours of Stoney's face.

Like it hadn't been years, Stoney took him in, sucked him in and made his toes curl. Stoney was still his lover, still knew what he liked.

Maybe Ford wasn't the only one who'd dreamed.

Maybe he was just starting to wake up.

Stoney took him all the way in, down to the root. Ford blinked hard, trying to process what he was seeing. Blond hair, plastered on Stoney's scalp, red lips wrapped around his shaft, the sight magnified by the sensation of Stoney's tongue dragging over the heavy vein underneath.

Ford panted, his asscheeks clenching. God, he was losing it. When Stoney reached up, cupped his balls in one callused hand, it was all over but the crying.

He shot again as if he hadn't come just minutes ago. His balls emptied, and Ford arched back until his head banged against the wall. Holy God in heaven. He swore he could feel every ridge on the top of Stoney's mouth, every bit of the length of Stoney's tongue.

When he could breathe again, he tapped Stoney's shoulder. "What do you need, baby?"

"I…." He heard their phones beep, in concert— Stoney's ringtone a donkey's bray and his a minion screaming, "Kum-by-yah!"

Geoff.

"Someone thinks it's time for us to make an appearance, I reckon."

"Uh-huh. Doesn't mean I can't make you come again if you need it." He wasn't going to leave Stoney wanting.

Stoney stood up, pushed up to give him a kiss that tasted like him.

He held on, not wanting to lose this moment.

Real life was waiting, right behind that door. Ford knew there would be a lot more of that than he wanted to admit.

"Can we, maybe, see each other tonight? After the feast and the feeding?"

"Yes." He kissed Stoney hard. "We can see all of each other we want. Ready to go get your thanks on?"

"Yeah. Yeah. I got stuff to be grateful for, I think. New stuff."

Damn. He sure hoped that meant him, not a half-dead horse. Ford rinsed them both off carefully, knowing they had to get out there and be family.

Stoney stole one more kiss before handing Ford a towel and grabbing one for himself.

They got dressed, and Stoney pulled those ridiculous socks back on. Ford popped the man on the ass, just loving the shocked look. "You look like a porn star, baby."

"You're a turd." Stoney's cheeks went bright red.

"Yeah." He paused. "You have any idea how tickled I am to hear you say that to me?"

"That you're a turd?" The shocked look made him grin.

"Yes. In that tone of voice. I missed you." Ford had missed this man so much, and now he needed to get to know Stoney again.

"Yeah. It was the hardest thing ever, walking away, but it had to be done."

"We'll disagree about that a lot, I bet. But right now, I bet your son is looking for you." They walked out together, and Ford decided why hide it?

"Daddy! You're wet!"

"I was taking a shower. What's up?"

"Geoff made horsey-overs!"

"Horsey-overs? My favorite!"

Ford raised his eyebrows. "What are those, Quartz?"

"Horsey-overs. The appetizers!"

"Duh, Ford."

Oh, he was going to beat Stoney's butt. Little shit.

"Oh! Horses' ovaries," Ford said, pulling out Ty's favorite joke.

"That's what Grampa says!" Quartz grinned up at him, and Ford had to smile back. He had to.

"What's your favorite one?" Ford asked. "Did Geoff make cheeseball?"

"Cheeseball and there's veggies and ranch and there's crackers and cheese and, oh! Sausage balls!"

"Did Geoff make anything he would eat, son?"

Quartz shrugged. "Does he still not eat cheese?"

"I'm not sure." Stoney looked a little worried. Geoff seemed to have a bit of a self-destructive thing.

"I'll ask him," Ford murmured.

"Thanks. He's going to fade into nothing."

"Really?" Quartz asked.

"Nope. That's just an expression, kiddo." Stoney was side eyeing Ford and nodding, though.

They headed for the kitchen, finding Angie there, boots off. "Hey! I'm in charge of stirring soup while Geoff goes potty. Wanna help, Quartz?"

"I do. How's Jellybean? Uncle Ford, Angie said I could name her."

"Jellybean, huh?"

"Yes! She's the color of red and black jellybeans melting together."

Oh, Lord. That was hilarious. "What's the soup?"

"Butternut and apple. It smells amazing." Angie handed Quartz the spoon. "Stir."

"Yes, ma'am."

"Ah, something Geoff can eat." Ford grinned.

"The stuffing has vegetable stock too. He'll feast."

"Excellent." Ford knew Stoney worried, so now he worried.

"Yeah." Angie rolled her eyes a little. "He gets down sometimes."

"We can cheer him up!" Quartz ran over to a stepstool and pulled open a cabinet. "I'll make his favorite tea."

"I thought you were going to stir," Angie said, and Stoney shook his head.

"I'll do it. Quartz makes the best tea."

Ford wandered, grabbing a sausage ball. "What should I do?"

"Grab me one of those?"

"Here." He snatched up another and held it to Stoney's lips.

Stoney opened up, and Ford heard Angie gasp. He didn't pull away, though. He had dick-all to be ashamed of. This was something he needed to start out like he could hold out, and God knew, half the staff was queer.

"God, that's good." Stoney hummed softly, and smiled. Lord, that was a fine expression on Stoney's face.

"Thank you." Geoff said it from directly behind Ford, the boo factor making him jump.

"Jerk."

"Boss, you wound me." Geoff clapped his hands over his chest.

"Geoff! I'm making you tea!"

"Are you?" Geoff smiled at him and Stoney before going to catch a leaping Quartz. "What kind?"

"Your favorite. The red box with honey."

"Oh, yum. You can help me make hot chocolate too, right?" Geoff asked.

"Uh-huh. I'd love that." Quartz hugged Geoff tight. "Make sure Daddy's stirring your soup right."

"I can see from here that he's doing great. Ford will help him."

Ford nodded, breathing deeply. God, the kitchen already smelled amazing, spicy and meaty and bready.

"It's going to be a good Thanksgiving." Angie sounded satisfied down to the bone.

"We have a lot to be grateful for," Ford agreed. For the first time in years, he wasn't at a fine-dining restaurant with the rest of the single-but-not-lonely crowd. The food was a little less gourmet, and he was in jeans and a sweatshirt, but he was surrounded by laughing cowboys, an enthusiastic kid, and one crazy vegan.

"Someone needs to rescue the cinnamon buns," Geoff said.

"I'm on it." He grabbed the oven mitts and pulled the doors of the big commercial oven open, the scent of cinnamon and brown sugar like heaven on earth. "Muffins, cinnamon rolls… man."

"Yeah. I thought we'd have guests, but they had to cancel, huh?"

"I'll eat them," Quartz said.

"Me too!" Tanner said, stomping snow off his boots. "Me and the boys are starving. Lord, boss. You order this snow shit?"

Stoney snorted. "Please do not forget that I am a Texan, born and bred. I had absolutely nothing to do with this nonsense. Blame Ford. It's his first year back home."

Ford chuckled. "I brought it from Santa Fe, huh?"

"Brought it from somewhere." Stoney grinned at him, lips quirking, and he wanted to kiss them, taste that smile. He didn't, because Stoney's son was right there, but he wanted to.

Tanner went to warm his hands at the oven, distracting him.

"Still got all your parts, Tanner?" Ford asked.

"Thanks to Geoff, yeah."

"He was trying to turn into an icicle. It wouldn't've been a bad look for him." Geoff pinked, but the expression was more pleased than embarrassed, Ford thought.

"Miracle worker. Do I smell cinnamon rolls?"

"Cinnamon rolls, blueberry muffins, sausage balls, coffee, and there's hot chocolate coming. It's a feast, y'all. We need to set a fire in the foyer too. It'll warm the whole place up."

When they put in the new meeting hall, it would feature a huge fireplace as a focal point. People loved that shit. Hell, Ford loved a ski lodge with a roaring fire. Maybe a little bar area. They were zoned for it, and they had their liquor license for when they served wine with meals to guests. Stoney and Ty had laid an amazing foundation. They just needed his contacts to move it to the next level....

"Dish up or get out of the way, Mr. Bossman." Tanner winked at him.

"Huh? Oh. Right. I was woolgathering."

"Planning his takeover of the world, more like it."

"Hey!" That was close enough to the mark that he flushed and resisted the urge to stick his tongue out at Stoney.

He stepped out of the way after stealing a cinnamon roll for himself.

Tanner dove in with his bare hands, the heat from the just baked pastry not even seeming to faze him. "Oh God, that's good shit. Pardon my French."

"The swear jar is in the pantry, Tanner." Quartz was going to put himself through college with the damn thing.

Tanner sighed but licked his fingers after plopping his roll on a plate, then moved to drop a quarter in the jar. He poked his head back out of the pantry, eyebrows almost at his hairline. "Someone have a bad day yesterday?"

Geoff blushed. "Shut up."

Tanner grinned over, shook his head. "Turkey."

"Gobble gobble."

It sucked that Tanner was straight in that boobie-boobies-boobies sort of way. Totally sucked, because Geoff was making goo-goo eyes at the lean cowboy. Tanner was a great sport, though, and Ford got the feeling Tanner would let Geoff down easy.

Some guys just had the worst luck.

Shit, who was he kidding? Up until a few nights ago, he would have counted himself in that number. Now….

Ford glanced at Stoney, who watched him intently. Now, he was lucky as fuck.

He shook his head and reached for a quarter to put in the swear jar without even thinking about it.

Quartz laughed. "You didn't say anything, Uncle Ford."

"I will." He'd have thought it, no question.

"Oh, okay." Quartz gave him a funny look, all crossed eyes and wrinkled nose.

Stoney chuckled softly, the sound intimate, warm enough that it made his cheeks heat.

"Okay, you bunch of ravening beasts. Get your brekkie and get out my way." Geoff held up his hands and roared.

Quartz giggled softly as Stoney came after Geoff with the spoon, waving it menacingly.

"Boo!" Tanner leaped out of the pantry, making all of them crack up.

Angie loaded up plates and such, leading the way to the real dining room. Geoff needed space. The man was in his element, the world condensing down to a single meal.

Next year, Ford intended to have a crowd, dammit. Something worthy of all this work.

Not that family wasn't important, but Geoff deserved to shine. So did the ranch.

Stoney touched the back of his hand on the way past him, and he tried not to jump. This was going to be an amazing day, one way or the other.

Ford found that he just couldn't wait.

Chapter Twenty-Two

STONEY stood out in the barn, looking over all the horses, safe and warm in their stalls. Thanksgiving dinner had been perfect—a veritable feast.

Now Geoff was ensconced with a bottle of Merlot, Angie and Hetty had headed home, and Quartz was playing video games after helping with the dishes.

He wasn't sure where Ford had taken himself, but he'd figure it soon enough. They had a date, right?

God, what a day. As if the storm was all Ford needed, the floodgates had opened up and there'd been touching and smiling and this quiet sense of them being a "them."

It didn't make sense, and he knew it couldn't last, because the thing that broke them apart hadn't changed one bit, but he'd take it. He would take the fantasy as long as he could get it.

Ford appeared out of the gloom, crunching through the snow. "I had to check on Jellybean."

"She's eating us out of house and home. I'm going to have to order more feed."

Think of the devil, and here he came.

"I feel like we all got extra oats today." Ford patted his belly.

Stoney caught himself reaching over, stroking the sweet, lean abs. "You have a good turkey day?"

"I did." Ford caught his wrist in one hand, fingers closing around it to hold Stoney close. "Did you?"

"Best one ever, to be honest. Feels like a dream, more than a little."

"You think so?" Ford chuckled. "I—thank you."

He wasn't sure what the thanks were for, but he'd take them. "Are you going to spend the night tonight? With me, I mean?"

"Yes. Barring any weird emergencies." Ford shivered, and they headed back for the house.

The kitchen was dark, and Stoney let Ford into his side of the house. Quartz was in his room, and they both settled in the family room, football that neither one of them cared about on the television.

Ford couldn't seem to stop touching him, fingers sliding on his arm, his thigh. They didn't say much, but they didn't get hot and heavy either.

They just relearned things like that Ford was ticklish in the curve of his elbow and that the roping scar in the webbing between Stoney's index finger and thumb fascinated Ford's fingers.

"Can we turn off the TV?" Ford asked, and Stoney felt a jolt of panic sizzle up his spine. What if that made things too quiet, too intimate?

"We can." He clicked the remote off, turned toward Ford on the sofa. "I don't want to fuck this up, you know?"

"I know." Ford sounded like he'd been gargling gravel. "I get that, baby. I'm worried I'll wake up tomorrow and be back the way it was."

"Yeah, except it can't be. Even if it's bad, it can't be the way it was. You know the truth about me and Brit."

"I do." Ford's eyes darkened to damn near forest green. "That took such a load off, Stoney. I swear."

"I'm a stupid fuck, but I'm not a bad man. I'm not a cheater. I'm not straight." Even Quartz understood that he wasn't like other dads. He wasn't ever going to have a stepmom. Never.

"I just don't get why Ty didn't tell me. Or Brit. I could have helped." Ford shook his head. "Probably good that Ty isn't coming until closer to Christmas."

"I don't know. Wasn't my place to ask."

"Why the fuck not? You put your name on his birth certificate."

Stoney shrugged, fingers tracing Ford's hand as he checked to make sure Quartz was still busy. "I was just being decent to Ty. He gave me a job when I needed one. It was just to keep this guy off Brit, and then...."

Then Brit died, and he was the dad. There was this beautiful baby boy who needed a daddy, and to be honest, there were days that being a good father was the only thing he did right.

"You're great with him. I can tell you adore him."

"I do. He's my son, and I don't regret a second."

Ford raised a brow, the beast stirring a bit, clearly. "Does that mean you didn't miss me?"

He thought about his answer, because he wanted to tell his best truth. "I thought that I was going to die when you left to go back to Albuquerque without me. Then I didn't die. I thought I was going to die when I had a baby to raise too, but I didn't. I missed how you loved me. I didn't miss trying to keep up with you, trying to be as good as you."

That was the best he could explain it, the best words he had.

"I'm sorry if I made you feel like you had to." Ford paused, obviously thinking over his words as well. "Though back then I'm not sure I could have been less competitive."

"I don't want you to be less than you are."

"No, I get that." Ford grinned. "You just have to know what you're good at. You're great with the guests, and you have a handle on daily operations."

He shrugged, smiled, but he didn't really know what to say to that. He was a cowboy. That was it.

"Hey. I mean it. I've learned a lot since I've been back."

"Have you?" He had too, honestly.

"Yeah. I mean, I still think we have to repurpose some to stay current, but it's about more than throwing money at stuff."

"I want Quartz's life kept basically as it is and to keep my horses." Really, when it got to brass tacks, that was what was important. His boy. His horses. The rest was details.

"Okay." Ford leaned close. "I want you."

"Good." He kissed the corner of Ford's mouth. "I still love you, asshole. I always have."

The smile that took over Ford's face nearly blinded Stoney. "Oh, thank God. I know it's crazy, but I love you too."

"Absolutely fucking insane."

"You owe Quartz a quarter." Ford chortled after he said the words.

Stoney couldn't blame him. The man had spent ten bucks on the swear box during the day. Angie and Geoff had done their best to trick him into an f-bomb.

"I'll give him a ten if you make love to me."

"Anything you want, baby," Ford said before kissing him hard.

He took the kiss, then locked up and led Ford to his bed.

Thanksgiving was turning out to be his favorite holiday these days, for sure.

Chapter Twenty-Three

THE open house barrcled down on Ford way too fast. With the snow, there was no way he'd get the road graded, and the office renovations had slowed to a snail's pace.

His contractor wasn't exactly cooperating. "Sam, I need you, not some assistant. Especially not a decorator...."

"Ford, there's no way we're doing major reno until spring thaw. The best thing you can do is have someone out to decorate the main barn that you want to make into the meeting area."

"There are horses in there."

"Then get them out."

"I can't just oust the horses." Ford chewed his lower lip. "Okay, send your guy, and I'll try to find him a space to work with." They had at least one large cabin they could clean out for a day. There'd be, what, twenty people at once? Tops?

The biggest cabin would hold the open house crowd.

"Will do, buddy. See you soon."

"Thanks, Sam." Ford sighed, clicking off his phone. On the one hand, life amazed him. He and Stoney were relearning each other, and Ford liked the man so much more than he'd expected to. On the other, his clients were going to start hunting his ass, and if he'd thought New Mexico was the land of mañana, Santa Fe had nothing on the Roaring Fork, where nothing happened until spring….

Period.

Stoney spent an enormous amount of time looking at Ford's marketing plans like they were albatrosses. Ford knew Stoney just didn't believe a gay-friendly space would work, but Ford knew from living in Santa Fe that it was an idea whose time had come.

For the business and for the community. He was home, for the first time in memory, home, and he intended to stay here with his family.

Ford took a deep breath before heading to the office, where he found Geoff with Mira. "Miranda? Is cabin one occupied?"

"Oh, boss. We've got no one but that pair of lovebird x-sport fanatics in cabin six. I'm not sure they're even still alive."

"Should I toss in a carrot cake and see if they bite?" Geoff had gained this new obsession with vegan carrot cake, and had made a new recipe every day.

Ford was fairly sure the raw food one had been a crime against humanity.

Who made cream cheese frosting out of cashews? Blegh.

"Mmm. Just don't toss it at me." Miranda almost kept a straight face. Almost.

"Hey, the last one was good!" Geoff protested.

"Which would be why I never tasted it." Miranda handed Ford the keys to cabin one. "Don't book it until after the thing, right?"

"Right on. What about the spring? Are we still booking then?"

"We are, but if we need to renovate, we can rotate. Right now we just have two families booked. Regulars, and, uh, friendly, if not family." Her cheeks heated, and Ford paused.

"Would it bother you? If we specialized in queer-friendly vacations?"

She shook her head. "No. No, I mean, I would worry that it would bother the clientele. I don't want to lose my job."

"No, of course not." Ford nodded easily. "No one will lose their job, I promise." If they failed miserably with his plan, well, he had a lot of investments he could cash in to keep them afloat until a new plan was in place.

"Cool. I'd love to have guests that weren't here to shoot things."

"Yeah. I mean, I grew up with the hunters." Ford knew they were mostly great guys. Still, he really wanted to move in a different direction.

"Meat is murder!" Geoff proclaimed happily, and Ford was tempted to punch him in the nose. Still, it was good to see the guy feeling less... what? Depressed? Down, for sure.

"I want this place to become a destination. Friendly, safe, upscale." Ford nodded and warmed to his topic. "Somewhere for weddings and honeymoons, team building, parties, and events for Aspen."

Geoff clapped his hands together. "Oh, man. I can totally cook for that."

Miranda bit her lip. "Stoney will still get to cowboy, right? And Angie and Tanner and Doc?"

"I want Stoney to have all the working ranch space he needs for his horses." Ford knew how important that was now.

"Cool, because you know how the boss is. There's never been a cowboy that needed a meal that was turned away." Miranda wasn't saying anything he hadn't figured out.

"There wasn't a cook that needed a job that was turned away either."

"Just no more raw carrot cake, please?" Ford grinned. Yeah, Stoney was a sucker for anyone down on their luck, but then he'd been there, right? Ford intended to keep that tradition going. Even though he still wasn't 100 percent sure why Stoney had been in a bad way back then.

Sometimes he felt completely out of step with the world. No one ever talked to him. He glanced at Mira. "Anyway, holler at me if anyone gives you crap about the cabin. Walk with me, Geoff."

"Sure, boss." Geoff twined their arms together and led him out to the covered walkway between the office and the main house.

"Okay, so I have to ask. Am I scary?" Ridiculous, maybe, but Geoff was so easy to ask this kind of shit.

"Scary as in serial killer or scary as in hideous beyond all reason? Because I got to say, that's a strange thing to ask."

He glared sideways. "Scary as in intolerant bastard who doesn't get to know what's going on in the family until it's too late."

"Can queer guys be intolerant?" Geoff teased, smiling at him before going serious. "This is about Brittany, huh?"

"So you know?" Did everyone?

"I'm her best friend's brother, man."

"Right. Wait. Wait. I thought…."

Geoff opened the kitchen door and pulled him into the warmth. "You thought what? That I was one of Stoney's rescues? I am. Stoney found me on my way out of town beat half to death. He didn't know me from Adam, and once he knew, he didn't give a shit. He didn't care I was gay, didn't care that my folks live on a clothes-optional, technology is the devil commune. Nothing. Once you find a place that loves you, you stay."

Ford nodded, but he wasn't sure he got it. Maybe that was it; maybe he was impossible to love. God, he was maudlin. "Yeah. I never thought I was that tough to talk to, is all."

"Right. Sit. This discussion requires tea."

They hit the kitchen, and Ford sat dutifully, folding his hands on the table to keep from fidgeting.

The kettle went on, tea bags plunked into mugs and cookies placed on little china plates. Honestly, Geoff was too precious for words.

Geoff sat across from him, waiting for the kettle, clearly, because no one began talking.

He let one eyebrow lift. Seriously, did everyone learn this quiet game from Stoney? He knew it wasn't genetically ingrained in the people from the Roaring Fork, because Ford could talk with the best of them.

Geoff still just kept quiet until the kettle whistled and the water was poured. "So, Brittany met this guy on a rafting trip, and they had a hot and heavy fling, which was great until it was time for him to go home to his wife and his job in DC."

Ford's eyes went wide. A politician? That didn't seem like Brit. Not at all. Not because the guy was wealthy, but because a Washington politician had to be older than God to a seventeen-year-old Brittany.

"Yeah. Well, think of the drama when she comes up pregnant. There's the freaking out, there's the whole publicity thing, and the man's wife? Desiree says there were Mafia connections. Now who knows what of the whole thing is true, right? They were teenagers. So was I. Maybe Brit was sleeping with some other guide and was too embarrassed to tell the truth. But she comes to Ty, and Ty went to Stoney, asking for a favor. Just put his name on the birth certificate. No one wants any money. No one wants anything but a name for this little one."

"Okay. I mean, I can see that, right? And I know this is making it all about me, but why not tell me when Brit died?" He could see Ty not wanting his still-in-law-school, crusading, liberal nephew involved if there was a GOP jerk that could screw up Ford's career involved, but after....

"Honestly? Ty shut down. He fell into the bottle for two years and didn't come out of the house. When he finally did sober up, Stoney had a two-and-a-half-year-old living in the bunkhouse and calling him daddy. Shame can make people do weird shit."

Ford sat back and thought on that while Geoff sipped tea. That was—well, it made as much sense as anything, even if it was ridiculous. Wasn't shame half the reason he'd stayed away from the ranch as long as he had?

And what about Stoney? Just raising this little boy, no questions asked, no hesitation? He'd been little more than a kid himself, and he'd manned up and been the responsible one. Sure, he'd ended up with half the ranch, but Christ, Stoney had earned every acre.

The sound of a sleek engine outside made Geoff start, but Ford just rolled his eyes. "Designer. Can you believe that's what Sam sends me?"

"She's got to be pretty studly, though, to drive up here in this crap. Lots of folks wouldn't."

"Yeah. Well, this is Colorado." He winked. "Thanks for the tea. You gave me food for thought too."

"That's my job. Feeding the world."

"Yep. Thanks, Geoff. Can you make sure there's more tea and shit for her after the tour?" He headed outside again, the cold stealing his breath.

He had to admit it was beautiful, though. The guys had the lights hung before the blizzard and now they shone and sparkled.

The sleek little SUV crossover also sparkled, and the man—not a woman—who stepped out of it was pretty flashy as well. And familiar.

"Ford! You have no idea how thrilled I am to get this assignment."

"Andy. Hey. Surprise, surprise." Hell, he didn't think Andy ever left Aspen. Damn.

"I know, right? It's like fate. God, this place hasn't changed in fifty years, has it? So very… rustic."

"I like the rustic." Ford knew if he was going to work with Andy, he had to start out like he could hold out and be damned firm. "I want to keep that feel but make it more luxe."

"Right. Tell me all your thoughts and plans."

Ford jerked his head toward the house. "Come sit in the office with me, and I'll run it down for you." There was no way he'd use Andy for the whole project. Sam had no idea they had a history, he was sure, but he just didn't trust Andy not to go all crazy on his ass.

For this one party, Andy would be great.

They headed into the main house through the foyer. Quartz was out riding snowmobiles with his dad this morning, checking fence, so there was no reason to wait on his partner.

"Have a sit," Ford said, indicating the chair across from his desk. All of Ty's paperwork was finally filed, the bookshelves filled with Ford's law books, the art on the walls his collection of Leland Holiday animals.

It was starting to feel like his home, especially now that one of Quartz's Ferris wheels sat on the floor next to his desk.

"How cute!" Andy exclaimed. "You do models for stress?"

"No, this is my nephew Quartz's work."

"Oh, he's talented. How old is he?"

"Nine." Young enough to be adorable, old enough to be a handful. Ford loved him almost as much as he loved Quartz's dad.

"Wow." Andy settled back in his chair. "So, spill. Tell me what you're imagining."

"What I need right now is a space to do an open house. I have a large cabin that has an open plan and a kitchenette, but I'll need solutions for parking and getting people from the office to the cabin, as well as a quick decor scheme that really illustrates what I want here." Ford studied Andy intently. Still really attractive with his pale hair and blue eyes, but he did nothing for Ford at all.

There had always been a wickedness in Andy, and five years ago, he'd found it clever and sexy. Now, he didn't think he would.

He was getting soft.

"And your intended market?"

"I want to appeal to a wide range of clients, including the families we've always had in. I want to expand to a more inclusive audience, though." Ford knew Andy would give him an honest opinion. "I want to make this an LGBT destination vacation."

Andy tilted his head. "Really? I can see it—you make it luxurious and classy, tone down the hunter chic."

"I want understated, though. Still a ranch. People can get slick B&B or hotel anywhere." He wanted comfort, wanted the cowboys to feel at home.

"So, for this party, do you want sparkles? More down home? Country Christmas a la *Little House on the Prairie*?"

Ford stared at Andy, letting the silence draw out until Andy wiggled in his chair, cheeks heating. "I want greenery and understated sparkle. Think Jackson Hole meets Santa Fe. My chef, Geoff, will coordinate with you on his menu. After I show you the space, he'll have tea for us."

"Sounds good. How many people? Do I need to focus on standing or sitting space and are you having a band?"

"I don't think there's room for a band. This will be a lot of chamber members and such, so we need to have some seating for the ones who don't get around so well." Andy did know his job once it got down to brass tacks.

"Have you contacted the chamber? Gay Ski Week is right after Christmas. This would be one hell of a place to have a celebration…."

"No." Heck yes. That was just the kind of lead building he hoped to achieve with this open house. "That's a great idea." Ford made a note in his planner. "Ready for the tour?"

"I am. I'm excited. You don't mind if I take pictures, right?"

"As long as they're just for the job. I don't have releases for everyone for anything else." He softened the words with a wink.

"I promise. This is just to make sure I remember the deets."

"Cool." The deets. God help him. He led Andy out to the cabin in question. Then he'd swing by the office with Mira before ending with Geoff.

The path to the cabin had been freshly shoveled and he made a mental note to say thank you to either Mira or Geoff or whoever.

The cabin was neat as a pin, and all the furniture was pushed back so Andy could get a good idea of the space. Someone had brownies hard at work.

Happy staff meant happy guests, wasn't that Stoney's position?

"Oh, this is nice."

Ford tried not to get all pissed that Andy sounded surprised. He'd had an attitude adjustment since he'd been here too.

"I want this place to be a showstopper, you know? Somewhere worth spending money at."

"I can see it. I can. It'll take work, but I can completely see it."

"Good deal." He let Andy wander to take measurements and pictures, standing back so he could see the big picture. Ford knew that was his strength. This cabin needed a loft.

That would be a perfect place for a band, for a second bedroom, or a place for someone to dress for an event. Maybe they needed to hide the kitchenette. That wouldn't be hard. Then they could really call it multiuse.

"…much work," Andy was saying.

"Huh? Sorry."

Andy chuckled, smoothing the front of his thin sweater where he'd unfastened his sleek ski jacket. "You have ideas. I can see the smoke. Talk to me."

"Oh, not for the event. Just for later on." Ford tried to relax; God knew he and Andy had always gotten along fine, so what was wrong with him? Well, there was that whole left him for a fifty-year-old sugar daddy thing, and Andy telling him he was staid and boring….

Still, now Andy seemed eager to work, to hear his ideas and plans, to listen to him, and for fuck's sake, Andy was his target audience, right?

"You got all you need? You still need to see reception."

"I do. I'm excited. There are so many options. Have you considered putting a loft in?"

"I was just thinking about that. Sam says no major reno until spring, though, so let's work on plans for that later."

"Right-o. Although if you hosted a ski fashion show for charity? Maybe a supper?"

"Huh. That sounds like a hoot." Ford nodded, mind racing. "I can see that. I'll talk to Sam."

"Good deal. How cool is this? To remake this place into something high-end? I love it."

"Yeah?" He grinned, warming to someone who could see his vision. "Now, the horse ranch factor still has to be workable. Top of the line. I'll let Stoney deal with that, but it needs to be on your mind."

"Are you planning a dude ranch type thing in the summers, or is this totally separate and we just need to gussy up the outside?"

"I think the ranch aspect is as important as the event destination. I mean, how many guys in Santa Fe have I heard say they wish there was a friendly dude ranch experience? No one will be kicking ass here, for sure." The queer folks outnumbered the straight ones on the Leaning N.

"I love it. So we need functional and luxe, all wrapped up together with an Armani bow and a lovely white wine spritzer at the end."

He tried to imagine Stoney with a spritzer in hand. The thought made him snort out loud. "You know I prefer a scotch and soda."

"I do seem to remember that. Me? I'm a Bloody Mary type."

"Spicy or not?" He knew the answer to that. Andy couldn't do spicy.

"You're a bitch." Andy laughed, though, and Ford nodded, grinning. Yeah. Yeah, he sort of was.

He led the way to the office building, where they both stomped snow off their boots. "Miranda? Got another minute for me?"

"Sure, Ford." Mira stood and held out her hand. "I'm Miranda, pleased to meet you."

"Andy Archer. Pleasure. I'm working with Sam Styles, the contractor. How does this space function?" Andy pattered on, and Ford checked out a little, grabbing his phone to make sure he didn't need to look in on either office.

Both offices' staff were beginning to panic, and he was going to have to head into Santa Fe sooner than later. Dammit. He didn't want to make the drive. Maybe he'd fly in.

Nah.

It was easier just to drive. He'd take the Interstate.

"We've lost him again," Andy said.

"No. I mean yes. I need to call Eileen. I'm sorry. Miranda, can you point Andy toward Geoff and the kitchen?"

"Of course I can. We're fine."

He nodded to her and headed out to his office so he could make some arrangements. He had a few guilty moments leaving Mira with Andy, but they were both charming professionals.

Now, Geoff? He would make Andy nuts.

Was it evil that the thought made him cackle? Yeah, okay, it did, but damn. He loved his life right now.

He wasn't sure how he'd feel about it once he got off the phone with the offices, but he'd take that chance.

Chapter Twenty-Four

"WHEN is Uncle Ford coming home?"

Stoney looked across Jellybean's back at his son, who was scowling, a hint of temper in his pout. "Tonight, he said. He's lawyering and dealing with fancy stuff."

"Fancy stuff?"

"Uh-huh. You know how Mr. Sam is here working on lumber and building?"

"Yeah." Quartz thought Sam was amazing. Absolutely amazing. He followed the big contractor around as if he were some sort of superhero.

"Well, your Uncle Ford is working with some guy to make it pretty and fancy for the big party." Some designer guy who probably hadn't ever seen a horse in person. Stoney had avoided the guy, because damn. He was fussy.

"I miss him. I want to show him what I did with his Ferris wheel."

"Tonight, huh? Geoff is even making pizza."

"Then he must be coming back!" Quartz hooted and jumped, which made Jellybean snort and toss her head.

"Easy. Easy." He was talking to both of them, wasn't he? "Shh. He'll be back, and we'll get ready for the party soon, huh? Only a couple weeks."

"No. Now it's a week and a half." Quartz always knew his numbers, and Stoney was surprised Ford had been gone that long. He was starting to wonder....

Except Ford called him twice a day and texted once an hour.

Some of the texts made his cheeks burn. He'd never had a... friend? Lover? Partner? A Ford to tease him. The things Ford wanted to do with him, with *him*, made Stoney sweat.

"Your face is all red, Daddy."

"Is it? Maybe it's hot in the barn."

"It's freezy!"

"Yep. I have Jelly Roll, though."

"Jellybean!"

"Jellyfish?"

"Daddy!"

"Peanut butter and jelly." Ford stood in the small side door into the barn, smiling, the lines on his face etched deep.

"Uncle Ford! Oh, we missed you!" Quartz hugged him tight, and Stoney loved to see that, how much his boy loved Ford.

"Hey, kiddo! I missed you too. So bad." Ford swung Quartz around. "How's Jelly Belly?"

"She's getting fat and sassy, Daddy says. Her coat looks better, don't you think?"

"I think she looks amazing." Ford came to him, arm around Quartz. "Hey. How's it been?"

"We've been busy. I missed you." *I love you.*

"I missed you too." Ford touched his wrist, the tiny contact giving him a thrill right up his arm.

His cheeks heated and his entire body lit up like it was the Fourth of July.

"Daddy, I think you might have a fever. Your face is really red."

"We should go get him some honey and lemon tea, huh? What else do we need to do here?"

"We were just brushing this little one out. She needs to learn that we're the good guys."

"Oh, so would carrots help?" Ford handed Quartz a Ziploc bag. "Start down there with Leonard and work up?"

"Yes, sir!" Quartz beamed, bounding down to the farthest stall, and leaving him with his lover.

"C'mere." Ford reeled him in for a kiss that damned near stopped his heart. His lips burned, the connection strong enough to make him dizzy. Yeah, someone had missed him, for sure.

They clung together a moment, panting.

"Hey." He couldn't stop smiling.

"Man, it's good to be home."

Listen to Ford calling the ranch home. Stoney couldn't be more pleased. "So, how was lawyer stuff?"

"Boring. I had to sit through three hearings on mineral rights. God save me."

"I'm sorry." That sounded like hell on earth. "The loft is damn near finished, and you got a wall in the kitchen now."

"Progress! How's Sam? Not killed anyone, right?"

"Nope. Not even that designer feller."

"Uh-oh. That sounds ominous," Ford said.

"Nah. You been dealing with him mostly. Sam, though, I keep hearing foul language about prissy designers." Stoney chuckled softly. He thought the whole idea of a designer, here, was hilarious, but Ford wanted it, so he was going along. He couldn't wait for Ty to see everything.

"Oh, God. He's the one who insisted, and the one who picked Andy. God knows I would have hired someone else."

"You know him real well?" They hadn't really talked on it. Once Ford knew he was fixin' to be out of town for a good bit… well, their talking had mostly been X-rated.

"I did once upon a time. We met in Aspen after I set up my office there." Ford made a face. "He was looking for more of a, uh, supporter."

"Like a sugar daddy?" Did people really still do that?

"Yep. Apparently I was neither a sugar nor a daddy." Ford shrugged. "He seems to be good at what he does, though, so I'll let it ride as long as Sam handles all the draws and such."

"I don't need a daddy, and I reckon him and me, we got different definitions of the sugar we want." He felt so damn bold, so daring.

"Yeah?" Ford's dark eyes went hot again, just for him. "I can give you some after supper."

"Geoff's making pizza." That made for spicy kisses, which stung just enough to make things tingle.

"My hero. I swear, if we didn't need him so badly, I'd back him in a pizza place now that Beau Jo's is gone."

"No way. He's ours, and we're keeping him." Geoff was the brother of his heart and the conscience of the Leaning N.

"I know." Ford winked. "We need to find him a nice boy."

"Yeah. Someone special." Not Ford. Ford was his.

"Yep. I'm glad you didn't fall for him. I would have had to kill him."

He checked on Quartz, then took Ford's hand, twined their fingers together. "Good to see you, man."

"You too, baby. I hear my Ferris wheel has been altered." Ford rubbed his hand, thumb digging in to massage.

"Indeed. It has lights now and a faster motor."

"Wow. I'll have to crow over that."

"One left for Bean!" Quartz said, bouncing over to feed the new mare.

She took it easily. Someone had taught her that people were good sometime in her life. Now they just needed to reinforce that. Remind her.

Stoney put Jellybean back in her stall. "Everyone have water? If they do we can go show Uncle Ford his wheel."

"Water. Hay. Sweet feed. Life is good." Quartz grabbed Ford's hand. "Come see now."

"Okay, kiddo. Show me." Ford winked at Stoney and let Quartz drag him away.

He watched for a second until Ford disappeared in the snow and the glow of the Christmas lights, then he secured the barn.

All was right with the world, at least for now. He guessed he'd take it.

Stoney headed up toward the house but stopped briefly at the office to check messages since Mira had gone home a little early.

That designer feller, Andy, was in there, working on a little laptop. "Oh! I thought you were Ford. That was his truck not too long ago, right?"

"It was. I think he's looking at his updated Ferris wheel."

Andy frowned, then made an "ah" face. "That cobbled together toy in his office?"

"Yes, my son made it."

"He told me. I suppose that's why he keeps it, hmm?" There was something smarmy about this guy tonight, something mean-spirited. Of course, maybe that was just the whole sugar daddy thing.

"Either that or because he likes it. Did you need something? I know Sam's already left for the weekend...."

"Geoff told me Ford might be back tonight, and I wanted to see him. I would have waited in his office, but I was already set up in here."

"Yeah. He's awfully particular about his office." Psycho, really.

"Oh, I know. When we lived together, I despaired of ever getting him a room that suited the design of the house."

Lived together? That didn't sound like what Ford described at all. Stoney went for blank faced on that. None of his business, because he knew where Ford was sleeping these days, right?

"I can tell him you want to see him."

"Would you? I have some decisions that need to be made for the party."

"Well, I can probably help."

"You? No. No, this is more suitable to someone that's more Armani than Dickies."

"Well, then." *Fuck you, asshole, and the horse you rode in on.* "Let me get the horse shit off my boots, and I'll fetch him for you."

"Would you? That would be great." Andy instantly dismissed him, turning back to his laptop.

"Yes, sir." Eventually. Once he got himself warmed up and he took his work boots off. Maybe had a cup of coffee.

He did love his evening cup of Joe.

FORD high-fived Quartz. "That? Is awesome, kiddo. I love it. The lights are just like a real carnival." He'd only been half an hour away as the crow flies in Aspen, but God he'd missed Stoney and Quartz and the bizarre cast of characters at the ranch.

With the weather and his late hours, he hadn't been able to come home every night and, to be honest, he needed to see his little Aspen condo. He'd told Stoney that he wanted to bring Stoney down for a few days, wanted to show his lover a good time.

Wanted to introduce Stoney to his colleagues.

Ford grinned. He wasn't sure Stoney was 100 percent in on that one, but he'd said he'd love to go to Aspen….

The main door in the kitchen slammed, and he heard Stoney stomping his boots. Ford's pulse picked up speed.

"I hear your daddy. Should we shut the lights down?"

"Yeah. When Daddy comes in, we all start making pizza."

"Sounds great." Ford carefully turned off the wheel, watching it slow and stop. Then he followed Quartz to the kitchen, his belly rumbling.

Stoney's boots were in the neat little holder on the way into Stoney's side of the house. No other sign of the man himself, and Ford felt a flood of relief when Geoff joined them.

"Quartz! My man. Come help me get the crust rising!"

Ford winked his thanks and slipped down the hall to Stoney's bedroom.

Stoney was stripped down to his jeans in the big en suite, washing up. The sight of the lean muscles working made Ford ache a bit with their sheer beauty. He reached out, hoping his hands had warmed up, because Ford had to touch.

"Mmm. Hey you. Feels good."

"Yeah? Not too frosty?" Ford hummed, stepping closer.

"No, sir." Stoney lifted his chin for an upside kiss, and Ford gave it, tongue sliding over Stoney's lips.

He did love the way Stoney tasted. Coffee and mint and spice. Ford had always adored that flavor. He'd never discovered it anywhere else.

"Uncle Ford!" Quartz squeaked to a halt in the bathroom door, eyes huge. "Uh—you—I—and there's Daddy and…."

"Breathe, son." Stoney straightened up, but didn't jerk away, didn't hide from Quartz's eyes. "What's up?"

"The man. The man is waiting for Uncle Ford. He says you were coming to get him."

Something very much like evil flashed in Stoney's eyes. "Did I forget? Oops."

"Oh, you're a turd." Someone was feeling his oats. Butthead. Still, the last thing they needed was for Andy to be bad-mouthing them to the organizers of the Gay Ski Week or the chamber.

"Am not. I get distracted."

"I can't help there." Ford grinned slow and wide. "Let me get rid of him, huh?"

"Please. Don't let Geoff invite him for pizza." Stoney winked, playing with him.

"No, sir. Andy hates pizza. I mean, who does that? Where is he, Quartz?"

"I'll bring you." Quartz waited for him to leave the bathroom, and then he asked. "Are you going to marry Daddy?"

"I don't know, kiddo. We're working on things, but that sounds right nice." The very idea made his cheeks heat and his heart race. They could do that now, for real.

"Okay. I'd like that, I think." Quartz sounded pretty at peace with the idea.

They walked into the kitchen where Geoff kneaded dough and Andy sat, glaring.

"Like what, little man?" Geoff asked.

"If Uncle Ford married my daddy."

Geoff chuckled. "Well, it would sure make things easier for those of us wondering which boss to go to."

"Turkey." Ford untied Geoff's apron strings with a tug, just to be a butt. "Did you want to go meet in my office real quick, Andy?"

"Indeed." Andy looked a little bit like someone had decked him—a touch stunned with a hefty addition of pissedoffedness.

Oh Lord help him. Ford smiled politely, waiting for Andy to get his shit packed up. Then he walked to his office, counting to ten so he could be prepared.

"Sorry. I'd asked Stoney to get you for me. I have some swatches and a few candelabras to discuss."

"Sure. I missed Stoney in the hall. What can I look at for you?" Ford kept his tone light but professional. Andy could just be grumpy because he wanted to go home.

"We need to talk paint colors first. I'm not sure the green we chose was dead on."

"No? I liked it." Ford was pretty set on the green, in fact. Understated but natural.

"Well, there's the sage we settled on, but there's also a coriander and a creamy mango."

Mango?

That was pink. Or was it orange. "What the heck color is coriander?"

"Sort of a sweet peach."

"Didn't peach go out in the eighties?"

Andy's mouth compressed into a hard line. "I would expect Sam to say that. You have more refined tastes."

"I learned to like real colors in Santa Fe, Andy. Let's do the green. It will be a good background for my Navajo blankets."

"You're the boss, of course. Do you want the decorations in a rich wine or a bright red?"

"For the ski party? Deep wine." He was still counting in his head. In Latin. "Candle holders?"

"What do you feel about installing a chandelier in the main room of the cabin versus floor candelabras?"

"As long as it's ranch friendly and doesn't foul the loft, I'm fine."

"It'll give an air of class, like crystal in a tent or something."

"Well, if you have something fancy for the party, we can rig the place for a wagon wheel or something, and you can change out the fixture for a special event." Oh, Stoney would love that. Love it.

"Hmm." Andy's designer savvy won out. "I like that idea. I can always wrap the chain to hide heaviness."

"Absolutely. Sparkly lights with those little crystals. Shiny is always good at Christmas."

"I have one I can pull out of storage."

Ford nodded. He was sure there was an upcharge for that, but he could live with it. "Cool. Anything else? You must be anxious to be home to… what was his name? Hiram?"

"Oh, honey, Hiram is so two years ago. I'm on the hunt for someone much more long-term."

"Well." Shit. He'd stepped in it. "Good luck, huh?"

"Thanks. Do you have any other concerns? We're heading into the last push. I'll be back up tomorrow to work."

"I feel pretty good. I'm here tomorrow, and then I have to run down to Santa Fe. I'll be back for the reception, but Stoney will be available to you and Sam."

"No offense, lovely, but the cowboy isn't the most fashion forward human being alive."

"Maybe not, but he's amazing with guests and reporters alike. That destination report we got in *The Sentinel*? That was all Stoney." Andy needed to remember that Stoney was his partner.

"Uncle Ford?" Quartz tapped on the door, offering him an excited smile. "Geoff said to tell you that dinner is in half an hour. I made your pizza for you."

"Thanks, kiddo." Ford stood, feeling a bit like a dick for not inviting Andy to supper, but knowing he only had so much time to spend with his family before he had to leave town again. It was too precious to lose.

"Can you see if Geoff has some of that white bean chili left to send home with Andy? You'll love it, Andy."

"Yes, sir." Quartz ran off, thundering away.

"Look, I'm sorry I'm not asking you to stay for supper, but I have a lot to catch up on with Stoney, and Quartz is so stoked about pizza night…."

"No problem, lovely. Seriously. I never thought of you as the… family kind. It's a nice look for you."

"I do seem to be settling down way better than I expected." Ford offered a genuine smile. "I'll walk you out."

"Thanks, I appreciate it. You want me to pick up something from Annette's for you on my way up tomorrow?"

"Would you bring some Kouign-amann for everyone to try? Expense it."

Geoff met them at the foyer. "Chili and bread, and some berry crumble for dessert."

"Oh. You are a great guy. Thank you. Seriously." And there was the flash of genuine happiness that had drawn him to Andy in the first place.

"No problem." Geoff waved and trotted off.

"Night, man." He clapped Andy on the shoulder before putting a hand on Quartz's shoulder. "Lead me to the pizza."

"Yay! I made yours. Did I tell you?"

"You did! What did you put on it? Snails?"

Quartz screeched to a halt. "Have you eaten snails? Like for real?"

"I totally have. More than once." He grinned. "Not on pizza."

"Ew. And my daddy kissed you. Ew."

"I like that way better than snails," Ford said.

"I bet he didn't know you ate snails, though."

"No? I'll tell him." He tugged Quartz into movement, his stomach growling.

"I bet you he won't never kiss you again."

"I'll take that bet."

"What's that?" Stoney asked. "Your Uncle Ford never bets unless he knows he can win."

His family was standing there, watching him—all of them, Stoney, Geoff, Tanner, even Angie and Hetty had heard that pizza was on the menu.

"I said you wouldn't kiss him no more 'cause he eats snails."

"Meat is murder!" He was going to kick Geoff's ass. No question.

Chapter Twenty-Five

"**I NEED** to speak with Ford."

"Well, that's just too fucking bad, man, because he's in court all day. What can I do you for?"

This Andy asshole was going to get himself beat half to death. The whole "Ford is the boss" thing was easy enough to deal with, because Christ knew Stoney gave less than two shits about whether or not the candles were ruby or scarlet, but this hysteria when he had a million things to handle—from the driving situation, to Geoff's meltdown over the fact that Andy put foie gras—who the fuck liked that shit at a half-bazillion dollars a pound anyway—on the menu, to helping Sam hang the new doors on the office and the main foyer and helping Mira figure out the new computer system for registration and booking.

Stoney had his hands full, especially since Quartz's teacher had just now announced she was pregnant and leaving once they found a replacement, Ty had announced that he didn't think he'd make the party, and Stoney was fairly sure he was about thirty unlistened-to voice mails deep.

This whole ski weekend party thing was going to kill him. If he didn't kill Andy first.

He kept reminding himself that the Gay Ski Week was a big deal to Ford, to this whole plan the man had to make this the Rainbow and Unicorn Dude Ranch.

"You don't need to be profane," Andy said, mouth tightening.

"No? Then quit pretending I'm the hired help and ask your question. I'm running harder than a two-legged greyhound."

"I need you to talk to your cook."

"He's not serving foie gras." If it was important enough to threaten to quit over, it didn't need to be on the menu. Geoff was the cook. He could make his own menu.

"Yes, well, he's changed the whole menu! This is not a barn dance. These are men with sophisticated palates, well traveled. Brisket isn't acceptable."

"It's a ranch. There's never a time in the history of the earth where brisket isn't acceptable." Besides, Geoff had let him try the little polenta cake with frizzled brisket yesterday.

That was what he wanted for his birthday every year until he died.

"But—"

"He's the chef. When you go to the CIA, you can make menus." Stoney folded his arms over his chest and stared. Hard.

Stubborn Texan cowboy was a role he'd been born for. Sort of literally.

"Ford is going to be unhappy if you destroy his party, you know. He's worked like a dog on this."

Stoney wasn't 100 percent sure he believed that. Ford had worked on the ideas and made decisions, but when drywall needed hanging or the drain in the kitchen stopped up, it was his ass doing the actual work. But whatever.

"Then he can take it up with me. He's in Santa Fe. He can't help you. You have to deal with me."

"I need greenery." Andy stared at him as if he could pull boughs of holly out of his ass.

"Okay. What kind?" He'd send someone with no real work to do to mangle greenery in the name of prissiness.

"Something like this." Andy pulled out a sleek smartphone and showed him a picture from some fancy magazine.

Huh. He was pretty sure that wasn't real. "That's something else. You want pine boughs?"

"Anything that smells nice."

"Got it. Anything else I can actually do? Geoff's off the table." Stoney needed to get back to work.

"I need to know the parking situation is handled."

"As well as we can. It's too late to grade the road. A lot will depend on the weather."

"These people will have sedans."

"Who drives sedans in the mountains?" Weren't these experienced skiers? What the hell?

"Most of these people. I tried to get a bus."

"A bus." *Lord.* "Well, I'll keep a weather eye out."

He'd have to think on how to keep all the fancy-assed clothes clean, he guessed.

"Well. If you hear from Ford, have him call me." Andy turned on his heel and left, and Stoney fought not to roll his eyes. At least Ford was returning Stoney's calls when he wasn't in court. That was doing better than Andy.

"Daddy! I want to go see Grampa!"

He frowned down at Quartz, who was covered in food coloring and icing and cookie crumbs. *Goodie.* "He'll be here Christmas Eve."

"You promised he'd be here to sit with me during the grown-up party!"

"He has dialysis, and I told you he'd try. You can sit and play videogames for a couple of hours." God knew Quartz tried to do that enough anyway.

"But!"

"Not now, buddy. I have a thousand dragons hunting my happy ass. You want to do me a favor?"

"Sure!"

"Go over there by the—" What was that fixin' to be? Something from a Stephen King movie or some such, even if right now it was a pile of snow with about ten thousand sticks with flags. Right. "—the labyrinth, and pick about a zillion pinecones for the party. Someone wants to spray paint them with glitter."

That lip began to stick out again. "Mr. Andy?"

Quartz was convinced Andy had run Ford off. Stoney didn't encourage the view, but he hadn't done much to help it either.

"Well, he's gonna do it, but I'm the one asking, and you can have them after the party, if you want."

"Okay!" Smile back, Quartz bounced off, and Stoney went to find Geoff, who looked a bit… tie-dyed.

"Cookies," Geoff murmured. "Gay skiers."

"Right. Remember, when the actual event happens, they want them again."

"Yep." Geoff gave him a hunted look. "That Andy guy…."

"I got it. I told him the menu is yours."

Geoff grabbed him and hugged him hard, heedless of his relatively clean shirt. "Boss. Boss, I swear, if you weren't my boss and taken and totally not my type, I'd kiss you."

"Shut up, butthead. Go make food."

"You got it." Geoff paused. "What do you want for supper? Anything I have in stock."

"Surprise me. Whatever there is extra that Quartz'll eat. He's in a state."

"No meatloaf, then." Geoff winked.

Stoney's phone chimed, and he grabbed it, relieved to see Ford's picture pop up.

"I'll be in the office, man." It was Ford's office, sure, but he didn't have one, and he needed a spot where he could talk and keep an eye out for Quartz. "Howdy."

"Hey, baby. How's it going?" Ford sounded so tired his words were slurring. Stoney knew better than to think Ford was drinking or anything.

"Been busier than a one-armed paper hanger. You?"

"Crazy. I didn't expect this dispute to go to court, and now the judge wants to hear all the testimony from the three other families whose well was tampered with."

"Damn. That sounds complicated." And boring as fuck, honestly.

"It's time-consuming." Ford sighed heavily. "Two more days, at least."

"You're going to…." Wait. Wait, the party was day after tomorrow, and Ford was at least eight hours away. "You do remember the party is Friday evening, right?"

"I do. I—I don't know, Stoney. I might not make it. Even if I'm done by noon, it'll be winding down by the time I show."

"But Ford…." No. No fucking way was Ford leaving him to deal with all these grand high muckety-mucks on his own.

"I'll try, baby. If I could reschedule either one, I would. Ty will be there."

"No, he won't. He's got dialysis Friday. There was some issue because of the holidays or some shit." He tapped on the window to get Quartz's attention because his son was wandering. "And Alanna just told me she was pregnant. Yay morning sickness, I guess."

"So we'll talk about putting Quartz in school. It might be good for him."

"What?"

"What, what?" Ford chuckled. "He's older now, baby. Maybe we can find somewhere private in Aspen that works for him, especially if we look for a program with lots of math and science."

"I—" No. No, he was the dad. He'd make that decision. Him.

"I think he needs more social interaction. This may be the best thing for him, you know? Open his horizons. I don't know. He's smarter than either one of us, that's for sure. He'll blossom, if we give him all the tools he needs. Hell, I'll do the looking into private schools, if you want."

"What about the party, Ford? You set this whole thing up." They had time to talk about Quartz, and he wasn't gonna do it over the phone.

"I know." Ford's voice took on a note of real regret. "I hate that I might not make it, but I need you to step up. Geoff has the food, and I know Andy is a trial, but he's a good planner."

"He's not you." He tapped the window again, giving Quartz the thumbs up. *Come on, son. Come in.* "He wants us to cut greenery and shit."

"Oh, for fuck's sake. He was supposed to get that, and he has a budget. I'll call him tonight if you want." Ford sighed. "God, my head hurts."

"I'm sorry." What the fuck was he apologizing for? His phone beeped, the texts coming in waves. He glanced at them—Miranda screaming about the parking and begging for help with the computer, Sam needing to know where he was, Geoff wanting to know where to have Quartz put the pinecones that wasn't in his kitchen, Tanner threatening to quit if Andy didn't get out of the barns. *Fuck a doodle doo.* "You sure there's no way you can make it in?"

"I'm going to try. Depends on the hearing and the weather. You got this, baby. Right?" Was that doubt creeping into Ford's tone?

"Well, Geoff's threatened to quit. Miranda's threatened to quit. Tanner just threatened to quit. Alanna did give notice, and Sam's waiting for me to hang a door." He was golden.

"Okay. Yes, sir. Hold on." He could tell Ford was talking to someone else for long moments. "Jesus Fuck. There was just a motion to extend to Monday. I swear to God. You're gonna have to pinch hit for me, Stoney. I'm sorry, but I need you to do this."

He closed his eyes, took a deep breath. Christ. Could he do this? All these fancy-assed folks who were going to look at him and, what? He was a cowboy without any pedigree at all. He didn't have a college education, he didn't have any real money, and he sure as shit didn't have the class that Ford brought to the table. He thought he'd be able to keep things working behind the scenes, smooth ruffled feathers and make the machine run like it was supposed to. He wasn't supposed to schmooze.

"Now you're mad." Ford could run hot and cold faster than anyone Stoney had ever met. "Damn it, Stoney, you can do this, and I need you to grow a pair."

"Hey. Hold up a second. You got no reason to be bitchy at me. I've been dealing with the mess you left me, trying to make this shit work. Don't you be all pissy."

Don't you fucking accuse me of dropping the ball, you fucker.

"I'm drowning in legal bullshit, and all you have to do is throw a fucking party, baby. I can't help but be frustrated."

"Yeah, well, it's your fucking party. Your idea. Do you have any idea how hard we're getting slammed since the ad ran over Thanksgiving? People are booking for—"

"Jesus Christ! Look. I'll tell Andy to deal with things, okay? You go feed horses or whatever, and we'll let him do the thing that's going to make or break this ranch."

Stoney's lip curled. He felt it, just pulling up in sheer disgust. Right. That was him. Feeding horses and living in the big house because he was raising Ty's grandson. "I got this. You do whatever it is you do, and I'll just muddle along as I do, right?"

"Fine. I'll see you Tuesday. I'll call Andy. Yes, sir, I'm on my way." Ford hung up on him, just boom. Nothing else.

He stared at the phone for a second, considered setting Ford's desk on fire for a heartbeat after that, but he settled on closing off the fancy side of the house and locking the door. *Fuck Ford and the horse he rode in on.*

Stoney headed out to hang the door, texting as he went.

Tanner: *You quit and I will personally beat you to death. Ride out and cut greenery.*

Geoff: *Put them on the back porch.*

Miranda: *Restart the damn program and call Mike the gravel guy.*

Then he called Sam. "I'm coming, man. Keep your damn pants on."

He would do this party, and Ford could stick the leftover greenery up his ass when he was sleeping on the couch Tuesday night. Stoney was so over this whole fucking thing.

Chapter Twenty-Six

FORD sat at the bar in the La Fonda, an untouched margarita in front of him. One of the other lawyers had bought it, clearly hoping to pry information out of him.

It hadn't worked any better than trying to get Stoney to answer his phone. So Ford worked his way through all his other calls, returning them.

He went with Andy first.

"Hello?"

"Hi. You called twice, so I guess it's important."

"Ford! Oh, thank you for calling back. You've left me in an impossible situation."

"Have I?" Great. Andy was in a mood. He could be a total sweetheart, or he could go on a tear.

"Yes. This cowboy of yours is—he won't work with me. At all."

"Andy, you can't order him around. He's not your assistant."

"I love how this is my fault. He won't approve the menu."

"That's Geoff's job." Ford rubbed his forehead, which was tight. "I told you, he's worth coddling a little. He's amazing."

"I want foie gras."

"He won't do it, and Stoney knows it. Just let him do his food."

"Then there's the construction. I was going to do something with the greenhouse."

"Not until spring. I swear to God, Andy, we talked about this. Sam would only do the cabin."

"Well, it's just like you to run off and not be here."

"What?" Ouch. Man, he was batting a thousand.

"You're not cut out for settling down on a ranch. I couldn't even get you to stay in Aspen. You kept going to Santa Fe rather than deal with me."

"Andy, I am not discussing this now. This is business."

"Yes, because God forbid it gets personal. You'll freak out."

"Oh, fuck you. Let Geoff do his menu. Use the space allotted."

"The parking. The weather is—"

"God damn it, ask Stoney. I can't be there."

"No, you never could," Andy snapped and hung up on him.

Ford growled, then called Stoney. Nothing. Geoff he simply texted and told to hold his ground.

By nine, Ford wondered whether anyone noticed he was foaming at the mouth. He gave up trying to call

Stoney and called Ty, instead, because he needed to fucking vent.

"Hey, Ford. I'm sorry, but I can't make the party. I told Stoney that I couldn't do it."

"Yeah, well, neither can I." Damn it, what had he been thinking, doing such a big event at the ranch before the place was ready for it?

"Wait, what? Why not? I thought it was this big deal for you two."

"It's a big deal for the ranch. Stoney doesn't seem so on board." Ford shook his head, then munched a chip with some salsa. "My settlement turned into a four-day hearing."

"That sucks, son. I hate to hear that."

"Yeah. I mean, I can't—" He stopped. Took a deep breath. "What if I fucked up, Ty? I'm not sure I can do both jobs."

"Then you need to tell those folks in Santa Fe that you're sorry, they need you at home."

"I went to school for a long time to do law, Ty." That was it, wasn't it? He loved the ranch, loved Stoney, but was he cut out to be an innkeeper? Really?

Was he really going to be a fucking dude ranch cowboy?

"Well, how can I help, kiddo?"

"Take the ranch back. I'll put the money into the repairs and consult, but you and Stoney could really make it new again." He wanted Ty to be at the ranch, wanted him not to be sick. Desperately. If he could go back in time….

"I can't. I told you, it's done. It's yours. You two have to learn to do this."

"I don't think I can." He felt sick, and he pushed away the margarita. "I fucked up. I know I did. I'm asking too much of everyone."

He didn't want to be a hotelier. He didn't want to do this—settle down and settle. Andy was right. He was incapable of emotional stability.

Oh, God.

"Ford." Ty's voice caught him, serious and sure. "You can, if you want to. But you have to want to, and you have to commit. It ain't fair to Stoney and Quartz for you to do this on again off again."

"That's why I want you to come back. I need you to."

"That's not going to happen. It's not on the plate. You own fifty-five percent. I'm not interested in buying."

All of the stress he'd been carrying since summer boiled over, and Ford lashed out. "Right. At least you're being honest about that. Not fair, but honest. Jesus, Ty, you spring this on me overnight, you don't tell Stoney…. What do you expect us to do? Why the fuck didn't you tell me about Quartz!"

"I…."

"What? You didn't trust me with that, but you'll trust me with your precious ranch? Fuck, I deserved to know that… shit, if nothing else that Stoney didn't cheat on me!"

"And you couldn't ask him?"

"No. No, I couldn't. I thought he'd taken my ranch and slept with my cousin."

"Then that sounds like you don't trust him, son, not me." Ty paused, breathing deep for a moment. Like a sick man. "I made a whole host of mistakes, son. A big old steaming pile. I let Brittany run wild, I let Barbara leave me over Brittany dying, I let you slip away. I miss my grandson every damned day, but I'm too sick to come home. Don't make the same mistakes I did."

He wasn't sure what that even meant. Which set of fucking mistakes was he supposed to avoid? He dropped his head in his hand, fighting pure hysteria.

"I can't even get Stoney to answer the phone, Ty."

"I can call him, but I don't know that he'll answer me. He's probably busy with Quartz."

"Sure." And he was sitting here alone in a hotel bar about to lose his shit.... What the hell was he doing with his life?

Maybe he just needed to go home, turn off his phone, and draw up the papers to turn the ranch over to Stoney.

The thought surprised him, but it made sense, in a weird sort of way. No more phone calls from Geoff or Andy, no more worrying about whether he could create this idea of a gay-friendly destination in a place where people came to be seen with a man who didn't want anyone to see him.

The more he thought about it, the more he liked it. He would back Stoney financially just as he would have Ty, but he would be free to live his life....

Stoney. God, he wanted that man.

He loved Stoney. He always had.

It hadn't been enough ten years ago, though. Love wasn't always the answer. Sometimes it was about doing what was right, not just for him but for the other people in his life.

Now he just had to figure out what that was.

"Ford? Son? Are you there?"

"I am. I'm sorry, Ty. I guess I'm just overtired."

"Well, get some rest. The party will go off fine. Stoney can do it."

"I'm sure he can." Ford wasn't sure. Not at all. Not least because every single member of the cast and crew of this party had called bitching tonight.

Except for Angie who might have been one of the people who'd quit on Stoney today and meant it. Jesus.

"Thanks for letting me vent, Ty."

"Anytime, son. I believe in you, that you'll make the right choices for you."

"Yeah." The unspoken idea that he would toss everyone else under the bus hung there, but Ford was too damned tired to fight about it now.

He just wanted to go home.

He just had to figure out where home was.

Chapter Twenty-Seven

STONEY tore the plastic off his best dress shirt, checking it over real quick before he tugged on his dress boots.

"Oh, you're wearing your fancy ostriches, Daddy. I love those."

"Thank you, son. You all set up for the evening? Geoff's going to be in the kitchen if you need anything, okay?"

"Uh-huh. When is Uncle Ford coming home?" Quartz looked so hopeful that he couldn't say the truth, which was he didn't know.

Ford had left a couple of messages, and then there'd been a text with "clear me half an hour Monday pls for a mtg."

A meeting.

You didn't meet with a lover who you had had a spat with, did you? You had wild make-up sex. You had a fistfight. You had a beer.

Meetings were for business partners.

Stoney fully intended to make things difficult as he could—through fucking or fighting or both—for Ford to take them back to meeting-together types.

"He's really busy, son, but I know he's wanting to see you soon."

"I miss him. I made him a cherry picker." Quartz was being so brave, his almost ten-year-old face set in determined lines. "Hetty said to text her if I needed her."

"Well, you save that for after Geoff and me, huh? She's with Angie in the barn."

"Okay, Daddy." Quartz nodded. "I have lots of episodes of *Elementary* to watch."

"My little detective. Wish me luck, son?" He undid his buckle, tucked himself in, and buckled back up.

"You'll be fine, Daddy. You're a cowboy."

"I am that, bud." He kissed Quartz on top of the head. "Okay. I'm off and running."

"Good ride!"

He nodded and headed out, straight into the kitchen, which looked like it was exploding with the sheer number of appetizers. "How goes it, man?"

Geoff glanced sideways at him, sauce smeared on one cheek. "I need a pair of hands. Do you think Doc or Doogie would come help?"

"You got it. The waitstaff are here and set up?"

"No." Geoff's mouth tensed. "The roads are a problem, boss."

"Okay, I'm on it." He stepped out the door and into screaming hell going on in the courtyard.

"Why the fuck hasn't this road been cleared?" Andy roared, and Miranda screeched back.

"Don't you scream at me, you asshole!"

"Enough," he snapped. "Mira, talk to me."

Andy opened his mouth, and Stoney just raised his hand, palm out. "No. Mira, now."

"The highway is clear, but from the main gate is impassable if you don't have chains. I tried to get it dealt with, but no one was available, boss."

"Ford wants—" Andy started, and Stoney shook his head.

"No, sir. I'm the boss. It's what I want, and right this second I want Tanner to run down and pick up all the waitstaff and get their asses up here. Next I need to talk to Angie about hitching up Barney and Fred, and Hetty needs to hitch Sally and Big Mike. Andy, you hire folks to deal with parking?" His brain was going a million miles a minute. Okay. They'd haul the folks up in the old sleighs, six at a time. Andy's parking people could get the cars lined up down at the main gate.

He turned on his heel, popping the kitchen door open. "Geoff! I need thermoses of hot cocoa in an hour! Quartz, honey, I need you to get your boots on and come help find all them fuzzy blankets that we put away last year."

"Yes, sir!" Quartz pounded down the hall to get his boots, and Geoff jumped to get pots of milk warming.

Tanner came when he texted and grabbed the keys to the big truck with the camper shell. "Back in fifteen with the waitstaff."

"Good deal. Then you'll need to saddle up for me. I'm going to play cowboy tonight for the guests."

"Anything else?" Tanner asked.

"Send Doogie up to help Geoff."

"You got it." Tanner disappeared just as Quartz came back.

"I'm ready, Daddy."

"Good deal. You 'member where all them blankets are?" At Quartz's nod, he smiled. "I want you to grab them and bring them to the utility barn, okay? We're running both the four- and the two-man bobsleighs, and there needs to be covers. You do it right and there's a twenty-dollar bill for you, deal?"

"Woo!" Quartz bundled up, and Stoney texted Doc to keep an eye on his kid.

"Do I get twenties too?" Geoff murmured.

"Shit, man, you get a Christmas bonus and a promise that I'll order in pizza for Christmas dinner." He had to tease. He'd cooked for Geoff once.

Just once.

"I'll get Quartz to make the pizza." Geoff's face twisted in a frown. "Have you heard from Ford?"

Conscious of Andy watching him, Stoney shut that shit down. "No. He had court through Monday."

"Damn."

"Yeah. He hates that he's missing this. Still, we have to make it work. I'll have Andy bring the thermoses down."

Andy gaped, and Stoney just ignored it. Everyone had to pitch in. He had to make sure the ladies used the fancy harnesses and to promise Hetty that he'd give Angie two weeks off over the holidays for her help. There was no one else he'd trust more to carry these folks up and down the mountain.

"Let's give these ski bunnies a night they'll never forget, y'all. I'm off to the barn. Geoff, no 'magic' in the coffee you'll do for anyone driving a sleigh."

"Got it. No Irish whiskey."

"Good man. Yeehaw, y'all. Let's make this the party of the season. We'll get Western on their asses."

Stoney would show them all how a Texan cowboy ran things, for once and for all.

Chapter Twenty-Eight

WHEN Ford made the turnoff for the ranch, he hit the brakes, surprised as hell to see several burly guys bundled up like Eskimos, waving him into a cordoned-off parking area.

He pulled up, cracking his window. "I live up there, guys. I got chains."

"Hold up, sir." One of the guys tugged out a radio. "Any sleighs on the road, Joe? We have a motorized vehicle."

He blinked. *Sleighs? What the hell?*

"Okay, sir. You're all clear. Have a safe drive up."

"Thanks."

About a quarter mile from the house, he started seeing the lights, twinkling like a million bright stars.

He could smell pinyon smoke as soon as he stepped out of his truck, and Ford heard bells jingling. Bells.

Angie and Hetty were standing holding thermoses with the sleighs and horses under the lean-to. They waved at him as he walked around toward the main house.

"Ford! You made it!" Angie called. "Stoney will be so tickled. He's been cowboying all night in his good boots, and you know he's frozen solid."

"Where is he? Over at the party or here at the house?" He needed to drop off his briefcase in the office, but he hoped to God Stoney wasn't hiding in the house.

"He's in the party. He rode each group of folks up. Then he settled in to show off his good buckle."

Hetty cackled, the sound merry as hell. "He asked us to stick around to carry people down after."

"You two are troopers. I owe you." He trudged through the snow, glad to see that mats had been laid out all over the courtyard between house and office.

He slipped into the main foyer, the door to his office closed and locked. He could hear Geoff talking, he thought, and he knew he heard Quartz laughing.

He'd peek in on them before he went to the party. Ease into things. Ford dropped his briefcase off in his office and locked up again. He went to his room and changed—pulling on jeans and boots and a jacket over a dress shirt. Okay, he needed some brisket and a water or a coffee.

He hadn't been able to wait until Monday, especially since his clients had agreed on a settlement. There was no way he could spend the weekend in Santa Fe with the papers he'd drawn up waiting in his briefcase.

Ford's hands shook when he let himself into the kitchen, the long drive and the nerves getting to him.

"Uncle Ford! You made it!" Quartz flew toward him, eyes lit up. "I helped so much that Daddy paid me forty dollars! Can you believe it? Forty whole dollars!"

"Wow." He grabbed Quartz in a hug. "You must be such a hard worker."

"I am. I'm just like my daddy."

Geoff grinned at him over Quartz's head. "Quartz! I need you to sprinkle chocolate chips on the parfaits. Three chocolate chips each, please. Hey, boss. You're home. We missed you."

"Did you?" Ford's heart ached a little, hearing that. "I'm sorry. Glad I made it. Can I have a nibble or two? I didn't stop to eat."

"You can have whatever you'd like. The brisket was a huge hit, by the by. Everyone loved it. Andy is going to eat his hat."

He wasn't sure exactly what Geoff meant, but he grinned and nodded anyway. It didn't really matter.

This would be Andy's last job at the Leaning N, he was sure.

"You have to try the pole-intra," Quartz said. "And the pickle-y onions."

"Okay." Ford stood there until Geoff guided him to a stool, then fixed him a plate.

"You look like poo, boss."

"Long drive." Long few days. It was going to be a long drive back tomorrow too. He might not survive it.

"Tomorrow you'll have to come see all the things I've built, Uncle Ford. I made you a cherry picker."

"Oh, neat. I went up in one of those once, when I was in college." Ford didn't explain that he'd been drunk at the time and trying to impress a guy. Or that that guy had been Quartz's dad.

"Yeah? I would like that."

A steady stream of waiters came in and out, taking plates and dropping empties off.

Geoff began sending desserts not long after that, parfaits and tarts and skier cookies with icing. Adorable. Ford was kinda amazed how smoothly the work went.

"Boss? Are you not going to go to your own party?" Geoff looked at him, those knowing eyes too old and too sad for someone who should be having such a good night.

"Yeah. Sorry, I was pondering a nap right here." Ford put on a smile. "Wish me luck."

"Best of luck. We love you."

"We love you lots. Don't forget to kiss Daddy hello!" Quartz laughed at himself, obviously tickled to death.

"I'll see you later, kiddo." He headed down to the main cabin, his feet freezing by the time he got where all the people were.

The crowd was sparkling and laughing, the music low enough to not interfere, but loud enough to hear. The cabin looked gorgeous, the lights and shimmer casual and classy at the same time.

He smiled as he looked around, desperate to find Stoney.

There. Stoney stood in the midst of a group of men, laughing, eyelines crinkled right up. He wore a shearling jacket over his good shirt and jeans, those ostrich boots dark with snow and mud.

He recognized the head of the Gay Ski Week committee, the brand-new organizer of Pride, and more than one of the men he'd met casually through his law practice in Aspen. They were looking at Stoney like he was a gay archetype come to life, as if Stoney was a fucking hero in a romance novel.

"He's amazing." Andy's voice shocked the hell out of him, coming from out of nowhere. "I'm serious. He just… came to life."

"I thought he was a classless jerk." Andy had said just that during their last phone call. Ford had to agree that Stoney looked amazing, making his heart squeeze in his chest.

"Well, he is a Texan…."

Ford snorted. "The place looks great, Andy. Really."

"Mmm. That was me. Getting everything else done, including getting your guests here? That was him. Totally hot." Andy grinned at him, one dimple showing. "Be careful, lovely. Tim Marrow wants to tie him up and keep him in a closet, and I'm fairly sure Mark and Dawson are considering stealing him and sharing him."

Oh hell no.

Ford blinked. Huh. With a visceral reaction like that, Ford had a hard time thinking giving up on Stoney was the way to go.

"I think I'd have to strike them down. A mighty smiting."

"I'd pay to see that. I'm going to check the bar. I'll be back."

"Sure." Ford waited for Andy to walk away, then studied Stoney again. Beautiful man, and clearly in his element. God, his world just kept spinning.

Ford walked closer, like he was drawn in by Stoney's smile.

"…idea. He's amazing, and I'm so lucky that he's my partner." Stoney's voice was warm, the drawl sensual and addictive.

"So, you two are…?" Tim Marrow's voice was partially shocked, mostly disappointed.

"Now, Mr. Marrow, it's naughty to kiss and tell. Y'all know that we're all family here, and we're so excited to have folks come and stay with us."

Ford blinked, then chuckled. This was why he'd fallen for Stoney years ago. That damned unassuming, wonderful charm. "Where have you been?" Ford murmured, amazed.

Like Stoney heard him, his lover turned, eyes landing on him. Ford expected coldness, rage, that emptiness where Stoney proved that, if nothing else, his idiot parents picked an appropriate name.

What he got was a surprised, pleased smile. "Ford! You made it!"

"Hey." He walked over to Stoney's side, the motion natural as breathing, and touched Stoney's hip, a brief press of his fingers. "Thought I'd surprise you."

He gave the men surrounding Stoney a rueful smile. "Wasn't sure I'd make it, and I didn't want to get hopes up."

"Well, you did. That's the important thing. Do all y'all know the brains behind the operation? This is my partner, Ford Nixel."

Ford shook hands all around, nodding at people he knew, getting names to go with other faces.

"I think Stoney here might be the brains, Ford," Tim said. "He got us all up here, and I can't imagine anything more charming than a sleigh ride."

"He's brilliant." He fastened Tim with a smile that wasn't all shark, honestly. "And taken. I'm so glad you all enjoyed the sleigh rides."

Stoney's chuckle was soft, low. "We'll be implementing them for the winter. An evening trip up to see the lights and to have a little magic hot chocolate and cookies from our chef."

They would, would they?

"We might have to try to steal your chef, boys," said a tall man with a sharp, attractive face. "He could really give the food and wine scene a go."

"You're welcome to try," Stoney said. "Geoff's not big on fame and fortune, though."

"He's a nut," Ford said fondly.

"He's our nut, and I reckon I'll keep him."

"Possessive man," Dawson teased. "Keeping Ford and the cook?"

Stoney jerked his chin toward the main door. "Doc is available."

They all turned to look at the grizzled, fifty-something cowboy, who was doing some sort of bizarre jig with one of the skiers from Austria or Germany or some such.

Everyone began to laugh, and Ford was so fucking proud of his Stoney that he could barely stand it.

Stoney winked at him, the expression in those gray eyes just for him, laser hot for a moment before someone else demanded their attention.

God, he felt like the world had pulled the rug out from under him again. He'd been so convinced on the drive up that he was doing the right thing, that it was time to walk away, and now....

Now it felt like Stoney wasn't just going to let him go.

As if Stoney was finally willing to fight for him, to reach out and grab what they could have, all he needed to do was meet the man halfway.

"I'm going to make sure that the folks that came from Denver are comfortable, Ford." Stoney touched his elbow. "Do you need a drink while I'm at the bar?"

"I would love something stiff." When everyone cracked up, Ford flushed, chuckling along. "Now that I'm not driving, I mean."

"It's good to be home." Stoney left him with the gaggle of men, who immediately began to joke and tease about how lucky he was, how he'd stolen the cowboy away from them and they hadn't even known Stoney was here.

"Hey, why would I share him if I didn't have to?" Ford protested, drawing more laughter. "Oh, I need to go say hey to Aaron Harris from the BLM. Have you guys tried the desserts and coffee?"

"Is there chocolate?" one man asked and another snorted.

"You're going to have to put in an extra day at the gym, Harry."

"Maybe two. It'll be worth it."

Ford steered them toward the parfaits before circulating some. Aaron from the BLM, Jeanne Fox from the chamber….

Before he knew it, Stoney was wrapping people in warm blankets and leading the procession down the mountain, chatting away from horseback.

Miranda came up in her glittery party dress. "The boss wanted me to let you know that there are a few people that shouldn't be driving and we are putting them in cabins and Tanner can drive them to their cars in the morning. Geoff wanted to make sure he could feed the servers and bar staff before they headed home."

"Absolutely. Can you make sure he has something more warm and filling than these nibbles for the wranglers and Stoney? Where's Quartz? Do I need to check on him?" Ford felt as though it was his turn to get busy and contribute.

"Last time I saw him, he was washing dishes for Geoff."

"Good man. Do you need me to glad hand anyone else, or have you got this?"

Mira was stunning tonight and looked to be on her game, totally put together as she nodded and smiled.

"Do we have contact information?"

"We do, as well as a lovely review coming in *The Post*, and we're trending on Twitter." Her voice dropped. "That movie star, Austin Neill? He was here with his husband, showing off baby pictures. OMG."

"Fucking A." He glanced around automatically for Quartz. "I owe him a quarter. Remind me."

"Will do. I'm going to make sure those cabins are set up. I'll see you in a few."

"Cool." Ford checked to see if he needed to schmooze, but the crowd was pretty much gone, a few stragglers meeting with Mira to get settled in cabins. So he headed back to the house, grabbing a tray of dirty glasses so he wasn't empty-handed.

The kitchen was raucous—waitstaff and kitchen staff and cowboys drinking and eating. Quartz was back in the corner, watching with wide eyes. Yeah, someone had had enough for one day.

"Good spread, Geoff," Ford said, shaking hands and thanking staff. "Hey, kiddo. I owe you a quarter." He held out his hand to Quartz.

Quartz took it and let him lead them into the quiet of Stoney's rooms.

"You okay? You did so well, huh?" Ford took a long moment to hug Quartz, that little body surprisingly strong when Quartz hugged back.

"Yeah? I helped?" Quartz leaned into him. "I'm so glad you're home. We missed you bad."

"I missed you too. I was worried I wouldn't get here in time." He'd been worried about a lot of stupid shit. Ford thought his New Year's resolutions all needed to start with "I will quit worrying about—"

"But you did."

The simple words echoed inside him, more than a little bit.

"I so did. You want to get a bath? I bet you got all sweaty in the kitchen."

"Can I wait for Daddy? I can play a game if you need to work."

"Sure. Did you get some supper?"

"Geoff made spasketti."

"Lucky man."

"Yes. I'll wait for Daddy to come. You can go have a kitchen party, if you want. Uh…. Geoff says Daddy needs warmer dress boots if he's gonna cowboy in them."

"Got it. We'll count his toes later and make sure he has them all." He winked at Quartz's giggle, then headed back to the kitchen.

Doogie, who was covered in flour and frosting, waved at him. "Good to see you, son. Want me to go sit with Quartz?"

"Would you? He's video gaming."

"We're buds. Besides, I owe him a butt kicking on Mario Kart."

"Thanks, man. I owe you all a bonus." He smiled, then jumped when Geoff poked him with a fork.

"Pasta?"

"God, yes." He took the spaghetti eagerly. "Andy still about?"

"I assume so, yes. He's probably changing up in the new loft."

"I'll text him. I owe him the rest of his payment." Ford grinned when Geoff rolled his eyes. He headed for his office so he could write a check.

He texted Andy and pulled out the checkbook from the locked drawer in his office. He could smell spray starch and Old Spice, and he knew Stoney had been in here. Maybe missing him.

He hoped that was it as opposed to Stoney wanting to tear the place down with his bare hands. Ford chuckled, sitting down and damned near breaking his tailbone on his briefcase.

It popped open, and the paperwork sat there, right on top. All it needed was their signatures and Miranda to notarize them, and he could walk away, go back to his perfect life in Santa Fe.

Except that wasn't his life anymore, was it? He'd sat in those hearings, worrying about Quartz not having a teacher and Stoney not having Ty, and missed his lover. He'd stayed in a hotel rather than go to his lonely, empty condo….

Ford grabbed the papers and headed for the great room, where a cheerful fire crackled away in the hearth, connecting the two sides of the house.

"Hey, Ford. Happy with the results?" Andy was back in his work uniform—skinny jeans and a turtleneck.

"I am. You did great, really." He knew there'd been a bit of weirdness with Andy being an ex, but the end result had worked out well.

"I did. I hope you keep me in mind for the rest of the remodel. I think I have your aesthetic down."

"I'll see what Sam says."

Andy rolled his eyes. "He'll say I'm a prissy queen, but I get results. What's all this?" Andy waved a hand at the papers Ford held.

It was a monumental mistake that he almost made, again. This time, though, he thought he wouldn't walk away and leave Stoney to his own life.

"I was going to sign the ranch over to Stoney." He grinned, remembering how Andy had always taken his freak-outs with a grain of salt. "I was being a panicky idiot."

"Love can do that to the best of us, or so they say."

"That's the damned truth. I figured it out in the nick of time." Ford tossed the papers into the fire, managing to hold on to Andy's check. "That one's for you."

"Well, I would have taken your half of the ranch, but this isn't a bad thing."

He smacked Andy on the ass. "Bitch."

"Yeah. We come in handy."

"You do. Thanks for everything, Andy, and I'm sorry if I've been an ass." He knew he'd hurt Andy's feelings more than once in this whole process.

"Working with exes is a bitch." Andy raised his voice. "Working with classless Texans sucks harder."

"Fuck you, Andy-o. Take your pansy-ass to cabin five, would you? I made sure to stop the toilet up just for you."

"Wow, you're a champ." Andy patted Stoney's arm on the way out of the room. "Great job tonight. For real."

"We do our best. Get you a plate of food and a drink from the kitchen, man. You earned it." Stoney looked across the room at him, snow still gathered on the plastic cover of his Stetson.

Ford waited for Andy to leave, to be out of earshot, and each tick of the clock was agonizing. "Hey."

"Hey, stranger. Welcome home."

"Thank you. I'm glad I made it. You were amazing." Ford just stood there, too utterly aware of the papers curling into charred embers in the fire.

"I.... Thank you. I tried to do you proud."

"You did." He held out a hand, needing Stoney to meet him halfway one more time. Ford took two steps forward, and Stoney did the rest, reeling him in. "I'm sorry I was a jerk, baby."

"You were, and we're gonna have to talk on it some, but that's what happens. People get out of whack and they have to get back together. I hate that back together means so many days in Santa Fe, but it is what it is."

"I freaked out." Ford leaned against Stoney, soaking up the hug he received. "I do that. Ty called me on it too. Told me to shit or get off the pot."

"You got a life there. I got a life here. I ain't never going to be classy, Ford. Or book smart."

"Stop it." This was Stoney's Achilles heel, just like second-guessing was Ford's. "You're capable and rock solid and mine." He kissed Stoney's jaw. "Quartz is waiting on you, and you need to change boots."

"Yeah. My dress boots are going to need some hard-core love." Stoney shot him a look. "My boots ain't the only thing that needs love, you know."

"I know. I plan to make that all better." Relief washed over Ford. They had to talk, had to hash out some of the issues, and he knew it. He'd rather spend tonight making love to his cowboy.

"Good." Stoney took his hand, squeezed it. "I'm gonna need you around some. This whole deal we started, it's fixin' to get big."

"I'm ready to commit." He brought Stoney's hand to his mouth, kissing those cold, rough fingers. "I'll call Patricia tomorrow to see if she's ready to interview some junior partners who can work the Santa Fe office." The more he said things like that, the more Ford knew in his soul he was doing the right thing.

"Tomorrow is the weekend, and we have plans that involve our bed, hanging out with a certain little boy, and possibly pizza." Stoney sounded very sure. "Call on Monday."

"Mmm. Pizza." Ford jumped when Stoney pinched him. "Ow! Quartz, save me."

"You're on your own, Uncle Ford. I'm on Daddy's payroll today."

"Traitor."

Quartz crowed. "Eat dust, Doogie."

"Well, I been beat again, fellers." Doogie climbed off the couch. "Got me a date with the hot tub. Night, you bunch."

"See you tomorrow, friend. Night." Stoney shook Doogie's hand and looked at Quartz. "Bath, child. You smell like food."

"I was washing dishes for Geoff."

"He told me. He's having himself a couple of glasses of wine and supervising cleanup. You're off work."

Ford leaned down, nuzzled Stoney's ear. "You know how hot it is, to watch you just take care of everything?"

Stoney shrugged, but the cheek under his lips heated. "I'm a cowboy. It's what I do."

"Well, I like what you do, baby. A lot." He couldn't wait to show Stoney how much. Soon.

As soon as he inventoried all of his Texan's toes and made sure they were all accounted for.

Chapter Twenty-Nine

"**GODDAMN** it, Ford! Where is that extension cord?" Stoney was buried under the second biggest motherfucking Christmas tree in the history of the earth. He assumed the one in Rockefeller Center was bigger.

He could be wrong.

"This is what you get for waiting until Christmas Eve to put the tree up, you know," Geoff said.

"I was waiting for Ford to bring up more lights since he used every single one of them for his party. Extension cord? Now?"

"You got it." Geoff handed Stoney a cord, business end first, thank God.

"Thank you. If this tree falls on me, tell my son I love him and Ford that I'm going to haunt him until the end of time."

"I got your back."

"Metaphorically," Ford said, joining them with a tote full of shit. "I hit jackpot in the attic, and Angie brought us lights."

"Good deal. Remind me why we're decorating this monstrosity instead of something less than eighty feet tall?" He was discovering he loved this—seeing Christmas through Ford's eyes.

"Because the last, oh, twelve years I've had a three-foot-tall fake tree in Santa Fe, which is one of the most Christmassy cities on earth. It was depressing. Is there eggnog?" Ford asked, poking Geoff.

"There is. Have you noticed that he completely disappears under there?"

"He's just wee. Baby, are you coming out before Ty gets here?"

Stoney was going to kill them both.

"No, I'm going to turn into one of Santa's elves and build a fort in here. Expect nuclear warfare before the New Year."

"Daddy! Grampa's here!"

"Oops. Time to put out the sugar-free cookies." Geoff pelted off, and Stoney thought he might just die in the tree.

Ford extracted him gently, turning him to kiss his mouth. "Breathe a minute."

"Yeah, yeah. Merry Christmas Eve, you giant butthead."

"You too."

"Well, now, it's cold out there." Ty walked in, Quartz clinging to him. "Feels good in here."

"Hey, stranger! You're looking good! Sophia must be taking care of your skanky ass." Stoney headed over to give Ty a hug, then kiss Miss Sophia on the cheek. "Quartz, can you take their bags on over to the big bedroom?"

They'd settled on living in what everyone still called Stoney's side of the house, and keeping a nice office and guest room on the far side. One day they'd give Quartz the big bedroom and move, but not yet.

"Yessir." Quartz beamed and ran.

Ford hugged Ty hard, then gave Sophia a gentler embrace. "Glad you made it."

"We are too. We're looking forward to seeing all your plans." Ty gave Ford a sharp glance. "Rumor is you hired junior partners for Santa Fe and you're not taking a lot of new clients up here."

"Word does get around."

Stoney looked closely at Ford, but saw not even a hint of panic in that much-loved face.

"I have to be here," Ford said. "This thing is going to take both of us."

"No shit on that." They were booked solid from New Year's Eve until June, and even if they managed to get the cabins remodeled faster than planned, they would have a yearlong waiting list by Easter. Ford's concept had taken off, and Stoney had been worried about their hunters, but two groups had already rebooked for November. They'd even brought on a specialized hunting guide and a permanent waitstaff. It was insane.

Utterly insane.

Stoney loved it. Every ridiculous moment.

"Have a seat, Ty. Sophia, what can I get you?"

Sophia waved a hand, her many rings shining, totally at odds with her flannel shirt. "I am going to bug Geoff. Need to stretch my legs a minute."

"Yes, ma'am."

Ty sat with a thud, gaze traveling up the huge tree. "Decorating late, I see."

"We've been swamped with a party, you know."

"Mmm. Well, glad it went so good for you." Ty nodded happily, a grin breaking out. "I was worried Ford would never get his head out of his ass."

"Look, old man. You just watch it." Ford flipped his uncle off. "You're still on my naughty list."

Ty sobered for a moment. "I did my share of screwing up, boys. Promise me you'll talk instead of hiding."

Stoney rolled his eyes. "All he's done is babble at me for a week. Lord."

Ford pinched his ass. "Bitch, bitch."

"What? It's true. The man never shuts up." And he loved it. Who would have thought that all that lawyering jabber shit would have a real use?

"Stoney tore me a new one too," Ford said. "You should hear him wax poetic about how he'd decided we weren't gonna have a business relationship, thank you."

Wax poetic, right. It was hard to do that when both y'all had your mouths full, but whatever. He'd got his point across clear enough.

"Good deal." Ty stretched. "Lord, I could use a beer."

"Which is why you'll have this coffee Geoff made you," Sophia said, walking back into the room, Quartz tripping along behind with a plate of cookies and spiced nuts.

"Oh, yum." He snagged a cashew and got back to work stringing lights on Gigantor the Demon Tree.

Ford chatted with Sophia while Ty napped, and Geoff's assistant, Tiny, came through with eggnog and such.

He scrambled up the ladder, then realized he probably should have snagged the topper on the way up. "Son, hand me the star, huh? I reckon I'll get that up, and then you can hand me up ornaments for the top."

"I made a potato gun, if you want to shoot it up there."

"Mmm. Little fragile for that." He winked, which made Quartz hoot. God, his boy was happy, which tickled Stoney to death.

"Here. I'll do it." Ford grabbed the light-up rainbow star, lifting it almost all the way up. Stoney reached, and when he did, he felt something cold and round pressed into his hand instead.

"Ford?"

The grinning asshole just nodded, and Stoney opened his hand to find a gold nugget ring with a chunk of turquoise embedded in the center. Solid, classy—it was a man's ring, something noticeable. A statement, Geoff would say.

A commitment.

"Wanna, cowboy?"

He looked down, and he nodded once, then slipped the ring on. Yeah. Yeah, he wanted. No question. "Hand me up that star, now. It's fixin' to be Christmas."

Ford laughed, the sound happier than any Stoney had ever heard the man make. "I know what I want under my tree."

"A pizza oven?" Geoff guessed.

"A new computer that matches the one I asked for?" God save him from almost-ten-year-olds.

"Nope. You'll just have to wait and see," Ford said.

He knew what Ford wanted, though. Stoney'd been under the darned tree all day.

What was a few more hours?

Coming in October 2016

 REAMSPUN DESIRES

#19

A Matchless Man by Ariel Tachna

Lexington Lovers

Growing up poorer than poor didn't leave Navashen Bhattathiri many options for life outside of school. All of his concentration was on keeping his scholarships. Sixteen years later he's fulfilled his dream and become a doctor. Now he's returning home to Lexington and is ready to prove himself to the world. In doing so, he reconnects with Brent Carpenter—high school classmate, real estate agent, all-around great guy… and closet matchmaker.

Brent makes it his mission to help Navashen develop a social life and meet available, interesting men. Unfortunately Navashen's schedule is unpredictable, and few of those available, interesting men value his dedication like Brent does. Brent's unfailing friendship and support convince Navashen he's the one, but can he capture Brent's heart when the matchmaker is focused on finding Navashen another man?

#20

Suddenly Yours by Jacob Z. Flores

What happens in Vegas doesn't always stay in Vegas.

Cody Hayes is having one epic morning-after. The hangover following a Vegas bachelor party is nothing new to him, and neither is the naked man in his bed.

His apparent marriage is a different story.

Carefully plotting every detail of his life carried Julian Canales to a Senate seat as an openly gay man. A drunken night of Truth or Dare isn't like him… and neither is marrying a man he just met. He'd get an annulment, but the media has gotten wind of his hasty nuptials. If Julian's political career is going to survive, he has to stay married to a man who's his opposite in every way. Now he must convince Cody that all they need to do is survive a conservative political rival, a heartbroken ex, their painful pasts… and an attraction neither man can fight.

www.dreamspinnerpress.com

Love Always Finds a Way

DREAMSPUN DESIRES
Subscription Service

Love eBooks?

Our monthly subscription service gives you two eBooks per month for one low price. Each month's titles will be automatically delivered to your Dreamspinner Bookshelf on their release dates.

Prefer print?

Receive two paperbacks per month! Both books ship on the 1st of the month, giving you *exclusive* early access! As a bonus, you'll receive both eBooks on their release dates!

Visit
www.dreamspinnerpress.com
for more info or to sign up now!

CPSIA information can be obtained at www.ICGtesting.com
Printed in the USA
LVOW08s1939111016

508344LV00001B/3/P